By CHARLOTTE AMELIA POE

The Language of Dead Flowers

Published by DREAMSPINNER PRESS
www.dreamspinnerpress.com

Charlotte
Amelia Poe

The Language of
Dead Flowers

DREAMSPINNER
PRESS

Published by

DREAMSPINNER PRESS

5032 Capital Circle SW, Suite 2, PMB# 279, Tallahassee, FL 32305-7886 USA
www.dreamspinnerpress.com

The Language of Dead Flowers
© 2022 Charlotte Amelia Poe

Cover Art
© 2022 Tylar Whitfort
instagram.com/tylar_whitfort_art/
Cover content is for illustrative purposes only and any person depicted on the cover is a model.

Trade Paperback ISBN: 978-1-64108-418-5
Digital ISBN: 978-1-64108-417-8
Published September 2022
v. 1.0

Printed in the United States of America
∞
This paper meets the requirements of
ANSI/NISO Z39.48-1992 (Permanence of Paper).

For Grace, who makes this world a better place just by existing and who makes me a better person by existing too. I love you, boo.
For Jay, who inspires me every day to challenge myself and to fight for the things I believe in. I eagerly await your video essay about this book.
For Aidan, you are the light of my life, and I am so glad I get to know you and watch you grow up. I love you so much.

ACKNOWLEDGMENTS

I would like to acknowledge the following people for being there for me throughout this process—you're all amazing, and I love you all so much.

Grace—I don't have enough words to say what you mean to me. This book wouldn't exist without you. You have been my most avid reader and most vocal supporter. You are so beautiful inside and out, and I feel so lucky to have you in my life.

Jay—you, more than anyone else, gave me the courage to write this. Every time I've been unsure of myself, you've been there and reminded me that I am good enough. You've been inspiring me for years, and I'm sure you will continue to do so for many more. Thank you for being my friend.

Tylar—thank you for realizing Tao and Adam and making them real people through your art. Thank you for being my spouse and for never, ever being weirded out by something I've said. I keep waiting for the day you realize you're too cool for me.

Reece—I want this in writing, in an actual published book, that you are the most talented writer I have ever had the pleasure of talking to, and I am in constant awe of what you can do with words. You're also an amazing friend, and it's just an honest pleasure to know you.

Mum—thank you for your constant support and love, even when I write books with somewhat niche appeal. The greatest gift you ever gave me was the ability to read and write, and I will never, ever be able to pay that back, except to say thank you and I love you the most.

To the editors who worked their magic on this manuscript and turned it from a series of words into something beautiful, I cannot thank you enough. I think, for the record, that Star Trek does exist in this universe. And to everyone who believed in this book and loved it and looked after it, thank you.

I listened to *Punisher* by Phoebe Bridgers on repeat whilst writing this book, so I should probably acknowledge that. I would also like to acknowledge you, dear reader, if you followed me from *How To Be Autistic* to here, because that's quite a leap you've taken and I'm happy you're still with me. Neat.

Finally, this book is for anyone who saw themselves in Tao or Adam and felt a sense of comfort. Writing this felt like coming home even though I'd never been there before. You are seen, you are valid, and you are so important. I want you to know that. It matters, you know? It really does.

Charlotte
Amelia Poe

The Language of
Dead Flowers

TAO

ADAM

CHAPTER ONE

DIRT—DIRT CHOKES Tao's lungs and blurs their eyesight, caving in as they run and scramble and try to free themself. Shards of white bone, ribs and femurs and thighs, hollowed out and empty, now scatter and trip them, and a skull, smiling and proud, stares up at Tao. A burst of blue flame, and it should be cold but it's artificially warm, not real fire, a shallow mimicry of it. A voice speaks words Tao can't make out, something about a boy, something about a boy who is important. A hand in theirs—they look down and it's a husk of a thing, withered skin and too-yellow fingernails. Eyes meet theirs and scream silently, and then the awful crack as the ground beneath them both dissolves, rips apart at the seams, and then the horrific march of boned feet on earth.

Tao wakes up, hits out at their phone as it vibrates on the bedside table just out of reach, misses, and then sends out an irate blast of energy that knocks it off and to the carpet, where at least its complaints are muffled. Tao leans back heavily into the pillow and sighs deeply, trying to get the taste of soil out of their mouth. It's the same dream, always the same dream, never any clearer, and gods, how they wish for answers. But there are none.

Well, perhaps there's one, but it doesn't bear thinking about.

The hands that raised the dead in the dream aren't Tao's. Tao is certain of that. They'd felt fear, not control. And Tao would never—

Tao slumps upright, stretches to relax clicking joints, and then swings their legs over the side of the small bed and plucks the phone, still vibrating, off the floor. It's just gone nine. Tao should be at work and curses at the realization. The dream sinks its claws in deep and refuses to let go. Tao's been sleeping through their alarm a lot recently.

They pull on jeans and a plain black hoodie, the holes in it seeming intentional but really just a sign of wear. They ruffle their hair, catch their fingers in braids they'd forgotten, and then spend five minutes they don't have carefully untangling them.

They grab a snack and practically inhale it, still chewing as they pull on their gloves and coat, and slam the door shut behind them as they leave their apartment.

"Terrible boy!" Old Luis yells at Tao from his own front door. His face looks like he's spent his entire life smiling and frowning, possibly both at once. Tao grins and turns on their heel.

"Not a boy, Luis!" they call, well-rehearsed in this routine.

"Terrible girl!" Luis parries back, and Tao grins wider and shrugs.

"Not a girl, Luis!" Tao replies, and Luis's face chipmunks with glee at this exchange—the same exchange they have every time Tao slams the door and Luis is around to hear it.

"Terrible menace child!" Luis says finally, and Tao does a little shimmy, points at Luis, and then grabs the handrail for the stairs and pauses on the top step.

"I try!" Tao says and starts taking the stairs two at a time, imagining the way Luis is fondly shaking his head.

Tao lives on the third floor and is more winded than they'd like to admit by the time they hit the street. They take a minute to let the noise of Nomos in while the slight ringing in their ears fades. There's the usual construction work two blocks over, a siren rings in the distance as the up and down of its drone fades into the background, and a child shrieks with laughter as her mothers swing her between them as they walk.

The city thrums with life, beating like the heart of a living, breathing beast, and Tao makes their way through it, brushing shoulders and avoiding people like it's second nature—because it is. This is Tao's home. They feel like they grew up here, the heartbeat of the city a part of them for as long as they've lived there, but it seems so much longer.

They hurry now, dashing across roads with a hope and a prayer, never stopping, because Zeke is surely already working his way into a fit at Tao for being late, and Zeke has that awful way of being *not angry but disappointed*.

But Tao still stops for coffee, but not from their preferred shop. Franchise coffee, bittersweet and warm as they take their first sip, the cold that slaps their cheeks momentarily held at bay with the plastic container held close in gloved palms.

Tao stands under an awning and allows themself a moment to watch the mad rush of late commuters and eager tourists and how the two types of people get in each other's way in complicated disagreement. The sidestepping and the grumbling and the small tripping of feet. The city dances in its own way, and Tao loves to watch it.

And then they're moving again, coffee cup ditched in a recycling bin and the world blurring as Tao approaches their destination. They skid down an alleyway that will cut a couple of minutes off the trip and then stop abruptly.

Their stomach turns, and the hairs on the back of their neck bristle. Tao feels the autumn chill and something else, something less natural.

The alleyway is full of recent death.

No—the alleyway is full of recent death and the stench of magic that comes with dragging a body back to life against its will. Tao closes their eyes and breathes deeply through their mouth, grounding themself, and lets the earth speak.

A body fell and then stood back up, corralled by forbidden magic, the kind that parents do not talk about in front of children, the kind that summons the police with a bullet to the brain without question or explanation.

Necromancy is forbidden above all else, and yet here there is proof of it.

Tao bites down hard on their lip as they reach deeper, trying to follow the path the body took—for it is no longer a person but a thing, something that once was and is again, but only just, something that will attack and maim and kill because it is told to do so. It is a weapon.

And it is in the city, somewhere.

Tao opens their eyes. Wherever the body is now, Tao can't find it, even though the death is still recent enough to sting, to reek and to remind. The city washes away all things in equal measure, and Tao is left adrift.

The phone vibrates in their pocket and shocks them back to life. With fumbling hands they reach for it, and it's Pru, warning them of Zeke and the impending storm that awaits.

Tao shakes themself to shake off the last remnants of death that cling oh so willingly.

They could—

They don't.

They could send out the smallest wisp of their own magic and fell the body wherever it stands now. Tao is strong—unpracticed but powerful. They have known their magic for a long time and known it was forbidden for even longer.

If they use it now, it would potentially, almost certainly, alert the other necromancer, and nothing good could come of it.

Tao likes their life, their job, their home.

Likes being a part of the city.

They sigh and start walking again, head and stomach churning, tongue tasting less like coffee now and more like ash. They leave the alleyway, and the miasma of death tries to follow but can't, the life of the city too vibrant for it to compete.

Tao turns a couple more corners and arrives at work. Fallen Gods Tattoos waits for them, the sign on the door turned to Open. The door is heavy as they step inside—old wood and glass—and it reminds Tao of something Luis would say—*"The bones are good."* This shop has been here for a long time, in Zeke's hands and in those of Zeke's family longer still. As long as people have needed protective charms etched into their skin, it has been here, where the spell writers and healers of the city gathered to create a sanctuary, somewhere that offers safety and the promise of protection—for a price, of course.

Zeke rises from where he's sitting, hunched over a desk, tracing runes onto transfer paper, privacy charm up, his customer watching with eager eyes, her hair in a ponytail to reveal the small shaved patch of skin that will hold the ink and then be covered once more. A little secret, like wearing a hidden locket around her neck, that will ward off most basic dangers—muggings, accidents, some turns of fate that even Tao doesn't fully understand. Zeke and Pru can craft pretty much anything, and how that works Tao doesn't know, doesn't know how the universe doesn't rebel against it.

"You're late," Zeke says, gravel-deep, as Tao shucks off their coat, hangs it on the peg, and then crosses to their station, gloves still on.

Pru pokes her head out from the back room, and Tao waves a greeting.

"Bad dream?" she asks, and Tao nods.

"Yeah, thanks for that," they say, and Pru smiles apologetically. Zeke's face changes slightly as a small frown appears on already weathered features and then disappears. Pru vanishes again in a flurry of blond hair, and Zeke tuts but gestures at Tao to sit and begin work.

Tao's first client isn't until ten, luckily, so they take a moment to soak in the atmosphere of the shop—the way the walls echo with wards and charms and totems etched so deeply into the bricks that it feels like nothing could harm them here.

They pinch their gloved fingers together, rub their first finger and thumb against one another through the wool, and wonder.

If there's another necromancer in the city, what does that mean?

Is it childish to want to pretend it all away? To go on as though they didn't happen across a life taken and then raised?

Power, Tao thinks. *This world is built on power—those who have it and those who will do anything to attain it.*

And in a city so full of potential, a hub of life and hope, power could be a very dangerous thing.

Tao shakes their head lightly, knowing Zeke is still watching, and gathers their supplies.

Who would I even tell? Nobody else will even know.

Because that's just it, isn't it? Only necromancers can sense the crimes committed by another of their kind. The rest of the world moves in blissful ignorance.

There's no easy answer, so Tao begins to sketch instead, hoping that this action, at least, brings more good than harm.

CHAPTER TWO

TAO WRAPS up their client and sends him on his way—a bouncer, wanting not protection at work but protection for his family, now etched into his skin as a buttercup on the back of his neck, covered by long hair. Then they throw away everything disposable, wipe down their station. Pru makes her way over, all under the watchful eye of Zeke.

"I really am sorry, for what it's worth," she says as she drags a wheelie chair over and straddles it. "Assuming it's my fault, of course."

Tao pauses. Pru seems tired, her eyes slightly tighter and more bruised-looking than usual. They shrug.

"It felt like one, a prophecy, but it was—gods, I hope it doesn't come true. It felt big, like it could devour the city. You haven't been having it too?" Tao asks, allowing her to scoot back as they spray disinfectant everywhere.

She shakes her head. "Nothing like that, no. Not that prophecy ever explains itself how you'd like it to," she says. "It's definitely one of the more vague powers to have. Utterly subjective, as far as I can tell."

"So the way it feels in my dream might not be the way it felt in someone else's? The things I see might not be what's actually going to happen?" Tao asks, hoping that their brain is playing games, seeing patterns in things that aren't there. If it's all subjective, then the prophecy dreams can be explained away as Tao's fear of who they are. Though... the alleyway. They didn't dream that.

"Definitely. It's very abstract. What's happy for me could mean disaster for someone else. And vice versa. Or I could read it as happy, and it could still be utterly destructive to me. It's like... an amalgam of experience, all shoved together into your unconsciousness. There's no reasonable hope of deciphering it and it actually coming true in the same way."

Tao pulls off their black nitrile gloves, snaps them into the bin, and pulls their woolen ones on again.

"Why do we do this to ourselves? Why do we keep ourselves open to this?"

Pru smiles a little. Tao likes her smile, though it's rarer these days.

"I think Zeke has the right idea, to be honest, with that block he's got. Mind you, easier said than done. I wouldn't know how to begin crafting one. Five years I've worked here and I couldn't tell you what he knows or what he can do. What he's picked up. He could be a powerhouse." She pauses, then looks Tao directly in the eye, her blue eyes burning bright. "That's why we keep ourselves open, though. Power. It's all about power. Nobody wants to be left behind."

Power. That's really what it all comes down to.

And raising the dead is the ultimate display of that—a violent disregard for nature's laws. Tao wishes they could tell Pru something, *anything*, but it's too dangerous, no matter how much they trust her. People react as subjectively as dreams do to bad information, and while Tao has never told another living soul, they can't begin to imagine the news being received well.

"I'm sure it's nothing," they say instead, knowing that it isn't, it can't be. "Hey, so, I'm going to get some hot chocolate. Do you want anything?"

Pru shakes her head.

"You can't avoid Zeke forever," she warns but smiles again. "He'll get you in the end."

"Maybe I'll bring him back a muffin."

Pru lights up with a giggle, because they both know how much Zeke covets the muffins from the coffee shop across the street. Zeke can be an intensely serious man, right up until he isn't.

"Okay, right. I'll be back in fifteen. Don't do anything I wouldn't do," Tao says and heads over to grab their coat from the rack. Pru salutes, and Zeke grumbles something under his breath about gods-damned part-timers.

The wind has picked up outside, and Tao sniffles as it hits their face. They cross quickly into the small, cozy coffee shop for hot chocolate with lots of cream and fifteen minutes to try to figure everything out without Zeke sending them cryptic glances. They get into line, not really looking at anything, just taking the room in, when they spot—

The most beautiful human being they've ever seen. Perhaps it's an exaggeration, but perhaps it's not.

He sits in a plush armchair, brown curls falling gently over the frames of oversized black glasses, a mug cradled in his hands as he stares directly back at Tao. He gives a little surprised smile when he notices Tao looking at him. Then he shrugs gently—a small offering—and tips his head to the chair beside him.

The brown eyes behind the glasses seem fathomless and deep, and the freckles on that cold-flushed face seem too adorable to ignore. He's bundled up in what seems like dozens of layers, and Tao thinks—warm. *Warmth.*

While Tao had hoped for a quiet fifteen minutes, this boy—for he can't be any older than Tao and he has the gangly limbs of youth still, wrapped up in a coat that seems to have too much fabric, scarf unwrapped and exposing a delicate throat—seems irresistible. Too good to be true, perhaps.

Tao knows people wear glamours and would have to get closer to be able to tell for sure, but it doesn't feel—no, this feels too natural to be store bought or even custom woven.

Tao orders and stands to one side as their hot chocolate is made, the fizz and hum of the machines quieted by the charms carved into their metal in neat swirls that could be mistaken for decoration but nevertheless hold the power bestowed upon them.

Soon enough, Tao has a mug of hot chocolate and a muffin balanced in their hands, and they look over at the boy, who again tips his head just so toward the seat beside him. Definitely an invitation, then, and one Tao's heart leaps at.

They settle in the chair, the cushions a perfect blend of firm and soft, no doubt brought about by some clever charm, and rest the muffin on the table. They take a sip from their hot chocolate and feel that instant burst of warmth blossom through them.

The boy places his own mug down and holds out a hand to shake. Tao doesn't take it, instead nodding and smiling. The boy drops his hand, but the smile that rests on his face doesn't dip.

"You work across the street, don't you?" he asks, then shakes his head. "Sorry, that was rude. My name's Adam. Sorry. I—I come in here a lot, and I've seen you go back and forth. You're a tattoo artist."

Tao's never noticed him before and looks Adam up and down, checking for glamours, but unless they're very good indeed, there are none. How had they never noticed him before? Something about him is familiar—familiar in a way that getting into an unmade bed is familiar, or shrugging on an old sweatshirt.

"Yeah, I mean, good eye. I've worked there about three years now. Still an apprentice, but you know, getting there," Tao says, takes another sip, and then mentally smacks themself on the forehead. "I'm Tao, sorry."

"We've got to stop apologizing to each other," Adam says ruefully, "but it's nice to meet you, Tao."

And the way Tao's name sounds on Adam's tongue feels like Tao chose it precisely to be spoken by him and him alone. Tao swallows the thought with another sip of hot chocolate.

"I can't believe I never noticed you before," Tao says, then cringes. "That sounds weird, but I just feel like I should have."

"I get that a lot. Don't worry about it. People say I just disappear into the background sometimes. Maybe that's my power—the incredible disappearing boy." Adam laughs a little uncertainly, something Tao can't read flickering across his face before it disappears.

"Well, I've noticed you now. And you've noticed me. That's… a lot of noticing," Tao says awkwardly, cradling their mug.

"Maybe because I wanted you to," Adam says. "Does that make sense? I was thinking, trying, well, trying to get my courage together to go and finally get a tattoo. And I knew you worked there, and I don't know, you always seem kind to the baristas, and you—yeah, it's dumb, but I thought I could trust you. Just didn't have the nerve. I like your tattoos, by the way."

Tao runs a hand down their face, from hairline to jaw, where Zeke and Pru's intricate handiwork intertwines beneath the skin— small marks and gestures that reveal nothing of the spells' intents but hum close and keep them safe nonetheless.

"I forget I have them, honestly," Tao admits. "They're so much a part of me now. But I can tattoo you. You should probably go to Zeke or Pru, though. I'm still learning. The shop—it's powerful but slow. Empathy only works so quickly, and it's very old magic."

Adam looks a little confused but seems to shake it off.

"I trust you. I said I did, didn't I?" he says.

"Well," Tao says, "I guess. I mean, I've got a free hour now. But it won't look like these." They gesture to their own face. "My tattoos, they can't be as subtle as all that. Not yet. They need the power that comes with being acknowledged. It… boosts them. Does that make sense? It's like a feedback loop—acknowledgment of protection increases the protection itself. And while Pru and Zeke can place all that power into a single line, mine aren't that good yet."

"So like the writing on the insides of these mugs," Adam says, because there's a small, cutesy phrase printed on the inside rim of each of their mugs, in a swirling font. Mechanical, mass-produced, and hardly magic at all, but it does what it needs to.

"Well, a step or two above that. Magic by machine rarely compares to handwoven magic, but I suppose if you're comparing me to, well, Zeke especially, then it's accurate, if a little disheartening," Tao admits.

"I always wondered what the writing in these mugs was for. Like, I know it's doing something, but I could never figure it out," Adam says, and Tao feels like they've missed something. It's obvious, isn't it? All magic, no matter how cursory, reveals itself by its own existence. The writing on the mugs offers a twofold charm, to keep the contents warm and to keep the mug from breaking. Tao knows that the second they touch their lips to it, the magic transfers through the self-same empathy that allows them to work in the studio at all or pick up Pru's prophecies.

"You really don't know?" Tao asks, baffled. Adam shrugs.

"I know I should. I've been told hundreds of times. I guess it doesn't come naturally to me, I guess."

A toddler should be able to pick up one of these mugs and know exactly what they were spelled to do, even if the toddler couldn't put it into words. It's innate, unstoppable as breathing. That Adam doesn't seem able to do that isn't just strange, it's alarming.

"You okay?" Adam asks, and Tao schools their face into something more neutral.

"Just realized I forgot something, is all. You still on for that tattoo?" they ask. Adam smiles wide again and tips back the rest of his drink.

"Yes. Definitely. Okay, before I wimp out again."

Tao drinks the last of their hot chocolate and plucks the muffin off the table, an important olive branch they mustn't forget.

Adam stands first and offers his hand again to help Tao up, but Tao pretends not to see it.

Adam shoots them a glance, which Tao might have missed if they hadn't spent their entire life noticing such glances.

Tao forces a smile, and Adam mirrors it. Standing, they're of a similar height, though Adam has a couple of inches on Tao. Their eyes meet, and Tao has the oddest feeling of déjà vu.

They must have noticed Adam before without realizing. It can't be anything more than that.

CHAPTER THREE

ADAM SHOULDERS open the shop door, holds it for Tao, and then steps inside. Tao looks at the studio through Adam's eyes, normally desensitized to it after years of working there, and it's pretty incredible.

It's old, but the ceiling is still high, and that leaves it feeling temple-like and as though it holds all the air in the world. The walls are covered in symbols and talismans collected over decades... no, centuries. Every time your eye rests on something, it's only for the briefest moment. Then it skids over to something else. And yet it isn't riotous or busy, but safe.

Above all else, this studio is safe. That safety is built into the very fabric of the building, and it emanates it in return, allowing Tao, Pru, and Zeke to do their jobs and to pass that security forward. It's the work of not one single pair of hands, but an uncountable number, forged through community. The same aspiration and goal have held steady for as long as this building has stood—to protect, always.

Tao drops the muffin unceremoniously onto Zeke's workstation, and Zeke looks at them, lets out a huff, and shakes his head.

"I want to talk to you later, kid," he says, gruffly but with warmth. Tao nods and walks back to hang up their coat.

While Adam fills out the necessary forms, Tao readies their workstation, sets out what they'll need, and grabs their sketchbook, not sure what Adam will want or where he'll want it. Some people like to hide their tattoos away, secrets that hang in the air and offer security through their invisibility, like a knife strapped to an ankle, waiting patiently. Others, like Tao, prefer to show their marks front and foremost, feeding them with other people's expectations that they'll work—the feedback loop they mentioned to Adam. Either method works, though sometimes Tao's work still needs that extra punch of being seen. There's power in visibility, in being a mark on otherwise unmarked skin.

Pru glances over from where she's working. Her privacy charm muffles her conversation with her client, dimming the sound of the machines too, but she looks between Tao and Adam and raises an eyebrow nonetheless. Then she wrinkles her nose, grins, and gets back to work. Tao doesn't respond, just reaches for their own privacy charm—a small opal stone, milky blue and brimming with power. They set it on their work table, beside the rest of their equipment, and feel the odd buzzing sensation take over as it hums to life, enveloping the few square feet Tao works in in relative peace.

Adam walks over, and Tao gestures for him to hop up onto the tattoo bench, which he does with ease, swinging long legs over the leather and drawing his knees up as Tao watches him. He stares at the sketchbook in Tao's hands, and he looks at ease, but Tao can sense the nerves vibrating off him.

Tao takes off their gloves and snaps on a new nitrile pair, making the transition as seamless as possible from years of practice. Adam watches but doesn't comment.

"So, what were you thinking, and where?" Tao asks and taps one gloved finger against their sketchbook while Adam thinks.

"What can you do?" Adam replies after a moment, and Tao grins. They open their sketchbook to the first few pages of ready-made designs—dozens of poisonous flowers and venomous animals in clear pencil-gray lines. Tao passes Adam the book, but Adam holds it between them instead so they both have a hand on it, holding it open. He raises a finger as though he wants to trace the lines but stops himself.

"Everything's so deadly," he comments, and Tao smiles. Not everybody notices, but some do.

"To be deadly is to be protected, right? It means people, well, anything, will take a second to think about whether they want to harm you. It's pretty brash as symbolism goes, but for now I need that. In a couple of years, I could do work like Pru—she's just over there." Tao gestures vaguely. "She can fit entire screeds of protection in a tiny line, because it's about intent, not design, but, well, for me, the design helps. And some people prefer that. They like the legibility of it. And that powers it, of course, because they believe it'll help them."

"Feedback loops upon feedback loops," Adam murmurs, still looking at the book in his hand.

"Yeah," Tao says, glad Adam understands, "all the way down."

Adam is quiet for a few more minutes as he flicks back and forth through the pages. But Tao notices the precise moment he makes a decision. Something changes in his posture; it becomes a little more rigid, a little more sure of itself.

"This one," Adam says, pointing to a ragged bouquet of wolfsbane flowers held together with a ribbon. "On my wrist."

"Are you sure?" Tao asks, though they already know. Part of this is always instinctual, the *just knowing* of finding what will protect you.

"Yeah," Adam says, certain.

"And is there anything in particular you'd like it to protect you from? I mean, I can do a general protection spell, but focusing on one thing can make it more powerful."

Adam bites his lip and puts the book down so the weight of it is in Tao's hand alone.

"I just want to feel safe." Adam glances around the shop as though he's afraid someone could have overheard. Tao wants to mention the privacy charm, but Adam should already be aware of it. Maybe something so sensitive could make him forget that, though. The words feel heavy in the air, like it's taken him a long time to say them. "I want to feel safe."

It's general in its way but also very, very specific. Tao knows more than a few of their own markings exist for precisely that same reason—the fear of something, or someone, or even yourself—the uncomfortable itch of powerlessness.

"I can do that," Tao says and smiles, and Adam softens again. "I can do that," they repeat, mainly to themselves.

"Cool." Adam pulls up his sleeve to reveal the delicate skin of his inner wrist, the purple of snaking veins beneath it, a tree that spreads out and always seems like it will break when Tao runs a needle over it. It never does. "Here," Adam says, though Tao already knows.

"Give me a couple of minutes to get it transferred?" Tao asks, already reaching for the paper that will take the design from the page to Adam's skin. Tao is already scanning which inks they'll use, each hand-mixed with different protective properties.

As Tao sketches the design over, Adam watches, and Tao finds it isn't as irritating as when other clients do it. Some clients hover, like they worry Tao isn't up to the task, as though Zeke would employ Tao for a single second if they weren't good enough. Adam, though…. It's kind of nice that Adam cares so much. It obviously means a lot to him that Tao gets this right. Adam isn't judging them. He's… interested.

Soon enough the design is transferred over to the flimsy sheet, and Tao asks for Adam's wrist. They disinfect the skin and prepare it so the design will stick at the same time. Tao positions the paper just so and then pushes down hard, and for a second, they can feel Adam's entire being pulsing through them, his life and heart and the blood rushing through his veins. It happens every time. The too-thin gloves don't offer enough of a barrier.

Tao's power begs to be released, to sap and to swallow and to leech. Tao quickly removes their hand and reaches for paper towels to smooth the design instead. There's a reason they don't touch people—the constant reminder of what they are and what the slip of a moment's mistake could cost.

They would never have picked this job in another lifetime, but they'd been desperate. It seems at odds, and they're all too aware of it. They just have to be careful.

Adam doesn't seem to notice. Instead he lets his hand fall loose and open as Tao pulls the transfer sheet back to reveal the purple stain that they'll soon be tattooing over. The wolfsbane bouquet looks like it was drawn just for Adam, the way it sits proudly on his wrist, and Tao is glad nobody else ever picked it out.

Adam looks down at it, twisting and turning his wrist just so to really look at it.

"You sure about this?" Tao asks, though they know. They're already connecting their machine to the power supply.

"Yeah," Adam says, sounding awestruck.

Tao asks Adam to place his wrist on the rest beside him and switches on their headlamp to better see. They smear a dab of Vaseline on the first few lines they'll be tattooing and, with their foot pedal, check the machine is ready to go.

"Ready?" Tao asks, and Adam leans back, biting his lip, face a little pinched but determined. He nods.

"If you need to stop, let me know. Even if you think it's silly. Just let me know," Tao says, buzzing the machine again, pleased that it sounds good in their hand.

With their other hand, they hold the skin of Adam's wrist taut, trying to touch as little as possible, feather-light but still oh so aware of the life Adam holds within him. Part of Tao wants to recoil at how intoxicating it is, to hold it within them and know what they could do. Another part wants to revel in the sensation, the fact that, while they could do harm, they never would. That Adam is worth protecting, even if it is just from themself.

They lower the machine to skin and etch the first line.

Adam watches the whole process with silent awe, and Tao soon loses themself in the familiar routine of it, careful perfection getting in the way of the *want-urge-need* that pulses through them to keep touching. *It so rarely feels this strong.*

If Adam notices how quiet Tao is, he doesn't remark on it, instead carefully reaching with his other hand to place an earbud in and fiddle with his phone until Tao can make out the soft sound of tinny music. They tune it out and keep tracing the lines, marking them permanently in black ink, pouring all the protective power the shop has given them into their actions, focusing on intent, the idea of Adam being protected, of being kept *safe*.

It's done all too soon, and Tao lifts their hands away, places the machine down, and both Tao and Adam stare at the tattoo. It's beautiful, more beautiful than it had been on the page, its stark black lines slightly raised and a little bloody against the pale of Adam's skin.

Tao wipes him down and quickly bandages the tattoo, brain on autopilot as they give out the aftercare instructions. Their hands want to touch more, to feel that vibrancy again, to soak in the sunshine warmth that Adam gives out even though he seems utterly unaware he's doing so.

"Hey." Adam places a hand on Tao's elbow and stops Tao in their tracks. "You okay?"

"I should be asking you that," Tao says, shaking their head.

"I know, but, well, you seem like—I don't know. I feel like I did something wrong and I don't even know what it was." Adam looks perplexed, studying Tao like a riddle he might solve.

"Just distracted," Tao says, which isn't a lie.

"Yeah?" Adam smiles. He smiles a lot. If Tao had a penny for every smile, surely they'd be rich soon enough. "Well, erm, I guess— this is probably.... I don't know. Is this okay? I wanted to in the coffee shop, but—I knew you'd be tattooing me, and I didn't want it to be unprofessional. But now I kinda… don't want to say goodbye. And I don't want to have to get a tattoo every time I want an excuse to see you. Not that that's what this was, but you know—look. I'm saying this all wrong. I wanted to ask you if you'd want to see me again, outside of work. Like… a date. If that's okay."

Adam blows out a long breath and covers his face with his hand, cheeks red.

Tao should say no. Tao doesn't date, because dating means touching, and touching is dangerous. Touching asks for more, makes their power pull at the leash and froth at the mouth.

"Okay," Tao says, surprising themself. "Yeah. But not today? I have… stuff. You know."

"Okay but not today. I can work with that." Adam smiles again, and Tao falls a little more in love. "What about tomorrow?"

"Tomorrow sounds good," Tao hears themself say. Just one date. Just one. And then they can go back to normal. One date won't hurt. No touching. Just talking.

"Oh gods, I need to pay you. I should have paid you first. Now it seems like I'm paying you to say yes." Adam sounds embarrassed.

"But I already said yes," Tao points out.

"You did, didn't you," Adam says, something akin to wonder in his voice.

I did. That same wonder echoes in their brain, continuing to echo as they help Adam pay and say goodbye to him and then watch him walk away through the glass of the front door.

"He had really weird vibes," Pru says, interrupting Tao's pondering.

"You think?" Tao asks distractedly.

"Yeah, I don't know, really weird."

"I liked him," Tao says absently.

CHAPTER FOUR

TAO SPENDS the rest of the day working with their last two clients, trying hard to focus on the task at hand and not either Adam or the necromancer plaguing the city. It would not do to taint a protective charm with wayward thoughts, so they do the best they can, promising between tattoos that they'll go back to the alleyway on their way home and somehow do some research once they do get home. They have no idea how to look up missing persons reports or if that's even a thing that exists outside of television, but there must be some proof that someone has gone missing. A life can't just be snuffed out without people noticing, right?

All the while, Zeke and Pru both send them different kinds of glances. Tao knows they have to talk to Zeke before they leave tonight, and damn, they know that will be hard. Pru, they want to avoid for different reasons. She'll needle away about Adam, and while Tao is sure she means well, it always comes off as slightly mean, the way she talks about some clients. She has a streak inside her that comes off as cruel at times. Tao is sure she doesn't mean it and knows for sure that she'd never let it influence her work, but still. Tao doesn't want to talk about Adam that way, if at all. It's another thing on the list of things to figure out.

The evening draws in dark and with gusts of wind against the sturdy thick glass of the windows, shaking but not breaking them, an ineffectual battering ram, the elements of outside versus the decades of peace that reign within the studio.

They clean down their station for the last time of the day, slip back into their woolen gloves, and watch as Zeke and Pru do their own cleaning, the heavy smell of antibacterial spray in the air. Tao runs a hand through their hair and fiddles with the split ends—dark and raggedy and in need of a haircut. They'll do it themself at some stage, because it's too dangerous to go to a hairdresser. Even that amount of touch is a risk.

What were they thinking, agreeing to go on a date with Adam? What was that strange, amplified sensation they experienced with every fingertip on skin while power rose up beneath their sternum and begged to be set free? It hadn't happened with any of their other clients, not in the beginning and not even today. Tao had always made sure of it, but Adam felt like a conductor, something beyond their control, something that amped up every itchy sensation beneath their skin and called for them to drain and to *take take take*.

It was unsettling at best, and what seemed all the more mysterious was Adam's complete lack of awareness of it.

"Tao!" Zeke snaps them out of their reverie and jerks their head upward toward him. He sits back in his chair and waits. Is there an easy way this talk can go? Tao hopes so.

"Good luck, little sibling." Pru wiggles her fingers at him as she heaves the door open to leave.

"Goodbye, Prudence," Zeke says, a warning note in his tone. She shrugs and lets the door swing shut, and once it has, it feels the same as when Tao set up their privacy charm earlier—that buzzing in their ears that promises nobody outside of this sacred space can hear them.

"Come here, come talk to me," Zeke says slowly, and Tao is reminded how ageless he is, how despite the lines on his face and the gray in his hair, he has never deigned to reveal how long he's had the shop or anything about himself at all. Even the block—the refusal to let in new powers—is strange and unusual and must have taken years to craft. Tao finds themself moving toward him and settles on the cleaned-down tattoo bench in front of Zeke. The power dynamic still makes it feel as though Zeke is looking down at Tao, even as he tilts his head upward to catch their eye.

"I've noticed you've been having trouble getting here lately, in the mornings," Zeke says, and that deep voice rumbles and does not judge. "I know you struggle with the dreams of prophecy that Prudence has given you."

Well, there's that.

"I would ask you to interpret them for me as well as you can, but know it would be meaningless for me to do so," Zeke continues. "Prophecy is an impossible power, and one I am happy to be without."

This is how Zeke reveals information about himself, Tao has

found—not by who he is, but by who he is not. A feedback loop with nothing to echo off, closing before it begins.

"I can show you how to build the block that would prevent these dreams," Zeke says, tapping fingers against the side of his chair, "but I know this is pointless. I realize you do not want to close yourself to these powers, and I understand. I was young once too." Zeke smiles, and Tao finds themself echoing it, though smaller and more unsure. "The time will come, though, Tao, when power becomes less attractive and more of a burden. We spend our whole lives accruing it, collecting it, and ultimately finding ourselves less certain than when we began. We start to forget who we first gained what from, and we realize that the empathy that allowed us these gifts compares naught to the empathy of the head, of letting people into our hearts, our lives." Zeke sighs, long and low.

"We live in a world that allows us to make these choices, though they do not seem like choices easily made at first. Certainly, it is easier to remain surface-deep and to take what is offered freely rather than to scratch that surface and to find the real connection, beyond power, that which cannot be used against another—no, that's not true. Empathy, real empathy, can be used to devastating effect should you want to do so, but one must hope that you do not want to. That love, platonic or romantic, will always hold your finger off that damnable trigger. This is what makes it so difficult, in a way that your collecting of powers is not—connection, true connection, is power beyond all understanding, and the costs and risks of it are more than we can truly bear. But the rewards—well, they outweigh everything. They *are* everything. What we're born to do. To matter to one another in a way that leaves us utterly defenseless."

Zeke stops, as though he's said more than he perhaps wanted to say. He hums under his breath, looks up at Tao, and waits for a response.

There are easy replies and there are hard replies, and Tao isn't sure which is which or what it has to do with them coming into the shop late. There's something deeper here, something unsaid, as though Zeke understands in a way Tao cannot. Tao feels very young, like a child asking their parent to explain something that seems infinitely complicated.

"I don't want a block," Tao says, because it's the one thing they do know. As much as the dreams plague them, they need to know what happens next, especially now. Any hint of the future is impossibly valuable, could stop something terrible. They can't tell Zeke that, though.

"No, of course not," Zeke says. "You are young, after all. But the rest?"

Tao shakes their head.

"I don't even know where to start," Tao admits. "I think I understand. I know there's more to life than power, but I don't really—it's not easy to let myself be vulnerable like that. You must know."

"I do, I understand. But may I suggest, this young man you tattooed today, and no, don't look at me like that, as though I've suggested you eat slugs or something silly like that—no, you listen, and listen well. Allow yourself to be human. Allow yourself connection. So many people in this world are lonely, and I see that you are alone. And these are two different things, but eventually they become one and the same. And lonely is a sad, devouring thing to be. So reach out. Allow this boy into your life. Live your life, Tao. Don't let it be a thing you *do*. Let it be what you *are*. Let yourself *be*."

It could sound trite, or overly simplistic, but it doesn't. Instead it resonates deeply. Is there a chance with Adam? Could they have something? If only there were a way to describe the sheer feeling of want they'd experienced touching Adam's skin through that layer of nitrile and how monstrous that made them feel. They wonder how they can possibly build anything when that power exists, craving and endless, urging them to destroy something— someone so beautiful, someone who has been nothing but kind. The boy who smiles. The boy with the wolfsbane tattoo on his too-delicate wrist.

"It's hard," Tao says, for want of anything else.

"It's supposed to be, at first. But after a while it gets easier. I promise you this," Zeke says, and he smiles a little, eyes crinkling.

"It happened for you?" Tao asks and immediately regrets it. Too personal, too close.

"Ah." Zeke takes his eyes off Tao's for the first time. "You see, when you are as old as me, you are allowed to make grand statements about what people should do, even if you never followed those statements through yourself. It's a different kind of power, granted only by age and regret. I could tell you of grand romances, except there are none. Of friendships kindled and rekindled through the decades, but that would be a lie. This shop is my greatest accomplishment, and even that is built on the work of dozens before me. But it has offered me salvation in ways I am lacking. I chased power because it seemed obvious to do so. Now I hand it back out, a gift. I keep people safe."

Tao wonders if that's how Zeke knows what lonely means. They don't know anything of Zeke's life outside this studio, but they'd hoped for something. A man so full of life, gruff but warm... there must be more than this.

"Don't be sad for me, Tao. Instead, I ask you not to repeat my mistakes. Make an old man smile. Grasp life with both hands; see what you can make out of it. Don't wake up in fifty years and regret. Don't be me."

"I thought you were just going to yell at me for being late," Tao says, because they don't want to talk about what Zeke's just said. How sad it has made them feel, for Zeke and for themself.

"That would have been easier, yes? But it wouldn't have helped. This, I think, has, though. Am I right?" Zeke tilts his head and looks directly into Tao's eyes as though he can see their soul.

"I think so," Tao says.

"Keep bringing me muffins." Zeke smiles again. "You'll find a lot of forgiveness through baked goods."

"Thank you," Tao says and means it. For everything. They think of Adam, blushing around his words earlier today, asking Tao to hang out. *Yes, even if it's scary. Perhaps* because *it's scary.*

"It's nothing. Now, get on home. It looks like it's about to start raining dragons and griffins out there."

"Those don't exist." Tao grins, hops down, and heads to the coat rack.

"One wonders," Zeke says quietly, and Tao nearly misses it.

"Hmm?"

"Nothing. Go home. And turn your alarm up," Zeke says, breaking that eye contact as he turns to put some equipment away.

Tao salutes lazily but with a mind brimming. The day is not yet over. There is research to be done, but Zeke is right, it looks like it's going to rain.

They should head home.

CHAPTER FIVE

TAO STARTS walking home, and the heavens open with rain that soaks through their coat and hoodie and to the bone. They quicken their pace, the rain muffling the sounds of footsteps around them, isolating them as they move through the crowds.

They reach the mouth of the alleyway, and something causes them to pause. They glance around, paranoid, feeling for sure that someone must be watching. But then they duck in.

The stench of death is still present, even as the rain washes it away. The sense memory of someone dying here and being dragged back is visceral and still turns Tao's stomach.

They crouch, pull off one glove, and press their bare fingers to the dirty concrete floor. Closing their eyes, they blot out the rain, the way their clothes are clinging to them, the sounds of people passing by. They focus on what happened, chasing the body that left here shambling.

They curse, for the first time, the limits of their power. While they can control it, they have no practice using it. They have been gagging it, and that leaves them at a disadvantage. They send out the smallest tendril—a beacon, hopefully unnoticeable—and wait for it to bounce back, a flare in the night that will tell them where the body is now.

Frustratingly, it bounces back almost immediately, seemingly muddled by the rain.

They send out another tendril, a little stronger this time, and feel the call echo through the ground they're touching and out into the city. Again, it bounces back within seconds.

They cannot find the body. They can't even guess where it could be.

Dejected, they pull their glove back on and stand, eyes still closed. Then they sway. It shouldn't affect them like this, shouldn't drain them so. If it were any other power, they know it wouldn't. But it's untested, new and imperfect, and lacks the muscle memory of repetition.

They open their eyes, and the alleyway looms tall around them, the fire escapes jutting out like rusted metal skeletons. The underlying stench of the dumpsters on one side forces them to wrinkle their nose. The rain keeps falling, and the world seems to close in, the sky dark and the alleyway darker still.

Whatever happened here, for now, Tao cannot trace it, and with every passing minute, it becomes less and less likely that they'll ever be able to. The fear rises again, that there is another necromancer in the city, that somewhere a dead thing is walking around, perhaps more than one.

Shivering, they rub their hands together and try not to think about the possibility that the other necromancer knows about them now, that the other necromancer could potentially trace them from those small tendrils of magic. They should move, get as far away from this place as possible, so they shake themselves and leave the alleyway, feeling the weight of eyes that can't be there on the back of their neck, feeling like they've betrayed someone they never even knew.

The rest of the walk home is miserable, and they don't even have time to ruminate on Adam and whether that's a mistake waiting to happen, all thoughts instead focused on the desperate need for a warm shower and the hope that the internet will reveal something about who this person was before they died.

How long before a person is reported missing? Has anybody missed them? Tao hopes so but then thinks, would they want to know? That someone they loved had become a husk of a thing, animate but no longer human, controlled and little more than a blunt weapon to aim and use?

They get to their apartment building, step inside, and breathe a sigh of relief. They pull off their hoodie as they trudge up the stairs, the events of the day hitting them all at once and making their movements sluggish and heavy.

As they reach their floor, Luis's door flies open, as though he is waiting for them.

"Terrible child!" Luis cries happily in greeting, and Tao can't help but smile a little.

"Hey, Luis," they say, and Luis taps his foot as though he's waiting for more. When Tao doesn't offer it, he tuts.

"You have forgotten our spaghetti day! My grandmother's recipe! You busy children with your busy lives. You do not remember the comforts of home that wait for you!"

Tao's life has become a *before* and an *after*. Before today, before that awful dream and the way it all spiraled from there, they *had* planned to visit Luis and eat the recipe Luis was insistent on teaching them—Luis whose powers are charmingly mundane but blessed. Good food and good company. Normally, they wouldn't turn down his spaghetti for anything, but today has just been too much. "I'm sorry, Luis," they say, and Luis looks them up and down, at the soaked hoodie slung over their elbow and the way their hair is clinging to their face uncomfortably. His expression becomes one of concern, and Tao wishes they could wish it away and make Luis smile again.

"It is okay, terrible child. I understand these things. Life, as they say, gets in the way of life. Perhaps tomorrow would suit you better?"

Tao nearly agrees but then remembers their promise to Adam. They shake their head, genuinely remorseful.

"Saturday, then!" Luis says, unaffected, the joy in his voice unwavering. "You will come on Saturday. Spaghetti Saturday—it is like it is made for it. You will learn this recipe, terrible child, and you will learn it well. I don't teach it to just anyone, you know."

And doesn't that just sting? Luis, who since Tao first moved in has taken them under his wing and become the closest thing to family Tao has. They are so, so thankful for Luis, his weird little ways and slightly overbearing personality. The way he jokes and laughs with them, but never *at* them. He is a rare and kind soul and one Tao is thankful to know.

"Thank you, Luis, and I am sorry. It's just been one of those days," Tao says, not wanting to explain but somehow sure Luis understands nonetheless. As if reading Tao's mind, Luis nods, satisfied.

"The days that we do not live through so much as they live us. I understand. Now, terrible child, drowned-rat child, I suggest a warm shower and some soup."

"Isn't soup for when you're ill?" Tao asks, not because they really care about the answer, but just to hear Luis talk, to hear his response.

"Sickness is not always visible, not always a cough or cold. Sometimes it is deep inside of you. Sometimes you do not even know you are sick until you are well again. Remember how it feels when you are ill and you forget the simple act of breathing through your nose. You do not notice the exact moment it changes and the act becomes simpler, but the shift still happens. I think perhaps you are waiting for that."

"I'm fine, I promise," Tao says, doubtful of it.

"If you say that you are fine, then I must believe you. But still, soup. And stop dripping on the hallway carpets. You know they will get grumpy with you! Get inside and get dry, terrible child!"

With that, Luis makes a shooing motion and his strange little face scrunches up, an admonishment. He then steps back into his apartment and closes the door, though Tao has the strangest sensation he's still watching through the peephole to ensure Tao does what he says.

So Tao does.

They shed their soaked clothes as they walk through their apartment and the wards welcome them home. Then they step into the bathroom and a lazy flick of their wrist turns the shower knob as they shuck off the last of their clothing. They step inside the shower, and the hot water feels scalding for a moment before they get used to it, and they spend a leisurely fifteen minutes untangling their hair and rotating slowly, gathering the water with their hands and letting it run through their fingers. Finally, when they can put it off no longer, they step out, the towel warmed on the radiator, and before long they're dressed in sweatpants and another large hoodie and settled down behind their laptop as it chugs awake.

Before they do anything, they reach for the fine silver Sharpie they keep on their coffee table, find an empty patch of black plastic on the laptop case, and painstakingly draw an eye looking back at them. Then, just as carefully, they draw a cross through the eye. It's crude, but it should protect them as they browse.

They load the browser, and their fingers hover over the keys as they try to figure out what to search for. "Missing persons" seems too broad, so they add the name of the city—Nomos—and press the Enter key. Thousands of results appear in less than a second, so they click the first site that comes up.

Snapshots of lives greet them—photos, descriptions, what the person was wearing when they disappeared. Tao finds they can search by location and narrows it down to the streets closest to the alleyway, but no results come back. They widen their search, but nobody's been reported in the last two days or even the last month. The body that waits somewhere in the city is as yet unreported, unclaimed.

They delete their history, just in case, and move to close the laptop. But then they pause. There's something else they want to look up. Something that's been bugging them since Adam first mentioned the mugs in the coffee shop.

They return to the search engine and type "adult no powers" and hit Enter. Fewer results than the missing persons search come up, which surprises them. While everyone is born with some ability, some power, there must be people out there talking about the possibility at least.

They click on a forum post and freeze when it loads.

The website has been seized. Bold black letters tell Tao that the authorities have claimed this page and hold it captive, that whatever information it contained was dangerous to public knowledge. Tao fights the urge to slam the laptop shut, lest some nasty little tracker charm find them, and instead clicks back to the next result, and is greeted by the same stern message.

They press a finger to the eye they have drawn and crossed out, hoping it's doing its work well for them tonight.

The rest of the results are the same through pages three, four, and beyond.

Any reference has been wiped straight off the internet. No wonder Adam talks so uncertainly about himself. If this is—if he really doesn't have magic, then he would have done the same searches. And found the same results.

Tao thinks about how both Pru and Zeke have talked about power in different ways and thinks about how there is power in knowledge and that those who control it and those who limit it could do real damage.

It doesn't sit right with Tao, not at all. Why would the government block this? It's a harmless enough question to ask, isn't it? And why not just hide the results? Why make such a display of censoring them?

Feedback loops. Uncertainty, then fear, then uncertainty. Ensuring people don't search any further.

Tao suddenly feels fiercely protective of Adam. They know how it feels to have a power they can't talk about, to potentially have no power at all and no resources to deal with that in a world that survives and thrives on magic.

It's a thought that sends a shiver down Tao's spine.

They think of Adam, the boy who is so trusting and just the right level of dorky, the boy who asked them out in stuttering sentences, the boy for whom Tao has already broken promises to themself and worries they'll break a few more.

Sighing, Tao gets up to heed Luis's advice and heat up some soup.

The laptop screen lights the empty room and ebbs out into the dark of the night through open curtains.

On the street below, a body tilts its head up and with white-hazed eyes makes a mockery of watching the window. Beside it, its necromancer smiles.

CHAPTER SIX

DIRT—DIRT CHOKES Tao's lungs and blurs their eyesight, caving in as they run and scramble and try to free themselves. Shards of white bone, hollowed out and empty now, scatter and trip them, ribs and femurs and thighs, and a skull, smiling and proud, stares up at Tao. A burst of blue flame, and it should be cold but it's artificially warm, not real fire, a shallow mimicry of it. A voice speaks words Tao can't make out, something about a boy, something about a boy who is important. A hand in theirs—they look down and it's a husk of a thing, withered skin and too-yellow fingernails. Eyes meet theirs and scream silently, and then the awful crack as the ground beneath them both dissolves, rips apart at the seams, and then the horrific march of boned feet on earth.

They recognize those eyes.

Tao jerks awake, this time before their alarm even has time to go off. It's the same dream—it always is—but something about it has shifted. There's a new familiarity to it that wasn't there before. They can put a face to the eyes they've been seeing.

Their alarm starts to buzz, but they swipe it silent. Brown eyes, normally framed with glasses, and the curls that fall into them—eyes they could fall into from across a coffee shop or across a dream.

Adam.

It'd be easy to hope that the dream has shifted because Tao has met Adam now, because Tao fell asleep thinking about Adam and what today would bring. And maybe that's true. Maybe that's all it is. Or maybe those eyes were always that shade of brown, and maybe Adam had always been waiting there. What had Adam called himself? *The incredible disappearing boy.* Unnoticed until Tao noticed him. What does that mean?

It's a bad idea, right? To spend any more time with Adam. Objectively. Because Adam makes Tao want, and that would be okay, but their power wants more, wants hungrily like an unfed dog bites and snarls, barely contained.

And Tao's never felt that before. Doesn't want to feel like that, like as much of a weapon as the necromancer they need to find.

The bodies that march in the dream cannot be the result of Tao's carelessness. That can't be what this is all leading to.

They get out of bed, and their phone buzzes as they dress. Once, twice, three times. It's Pru, still looking out for them, always looking out for them.

This is your alarm call.

Seriously, Zeke will be pissed if you show up late again.

Little sibling, little sibling, don't be late. I can't always protect you.

But there's a thought, right?

It comes to Tao as they stare into the mirror and their protective tattoos stare back at them, dark marks on tan skin. Protection comes in many forms. Surely there must be a form of protection against one-self, a way of making it so you do no harm.

Tao makes a mental note to ask Pru when they get to the shop. Maybe, hopefully, there'll be time to add a quick tattoo to their collection before they see Adam. They haven't heard of it being done before, because the people who do harm don't normally want to be constrained. But it must at least be possible.

Tao eats at their small makeshift breakfast table/desk and scrolls through their phone with one hand as they search for protective tattoos in the vein of what they're thinking, cereal growing soggy and unappetizing as they do. They choke as much of it down as they can before they grab their coat and head out.

The streets smell of fresh rain. More must have fallen after Tao fell asleep last night, and despite the night of restless dreaming, Tao feels awake as a result of the brisk cool air. There's a bite of something they can't quite place as they walk the familiar path to the tattoo studio, this time avoiding the alleyway entirely, knowing they'll find nothing good or helpful there. It feels as though they're walking in echoes, and that's entirely possible. Many people must walk this same path every day, but this feels more deliberate. Tao tries to push it from their mind; they're just getting paranoid.

They shoulder the heavy shop door open, and Pru almost falls upon them. She wraps arms around Tao in glee at Tao being early.

"Little sibling!" she cries, and Tao shrugs her off, unenthusiastic about the way she clings to them. She lets go, and they shrug off their coat, wishing they hadn't been too distracted to stop for coffee.

"Pru," Tao says and then really looks at her. She seems exhausted, more so than yesterday. "You okay?"

"My personal life is a disaster, little sibling," Pru declares, and they walk through the shop toward her station. Pru drags a chair with her, apparently so Tao can sit and chat.

Tao sits on one side of the tattoo bench, and Pru sits on the other, the divide oddly forbidding. Pru rests her arms on the leather, stretches them straight out, and crosses them at the wrists.

"Is there anything I can do to help?" Tao asks when she yawns and doesn't even attempt to cover it, mouth wide and shark-teeth white.

"Oh, that'd be nice, wouldn't it, but no," she says and smiles. Her smiles always veer closer to smirks than true smiles, but Tao still counts them. "I'm simply tired of being underestimated by people. By people not seeing me. And sadly, I don't think there's anything you can do to fix that." She raps her nails on the leather, dull little taps that are barely there.

"I'm sorry," Tao says, not sure what she wants them to say, but the way she scans their face makes it feel like she's looking for something.

"Yes, well. We can't all have cute little hipsters asking us out on dates, can we? How is your boy with the strange vibes and silly hair?"

Unnecessarily biting, but Pru's way. Tao tries not to take it personally for their sake or for Adam's.

"We're hanging out tonight, after work. Though I'm not entirely sure where I'm supposed to meet him—here, I suppose—or what we'll be doing." And Tao realizes how little they actually planned it yesterday, caught up in the mad rush of each other.

"Sickening," Pru says, wrinkling her nose. "I still don't like him."

Tao doesn't understand why not, but Pru often works like that, basing decisions on feelings and aspersions she has cast far more freely than Tao might.

"Hey, Pru?" Tao asks, remembering what they meant to ask her. "Could you tattoo me later if you have time?"

She perks up at this, having been staring at her nails.

"Of course! What were you thinking? Something to woo this boy? A little glamour between friends?" She practically purrs, and Tao wishes she were a little less, well, her. But then she wouldn't be Pru, and despite everything, she's been a good friend. She took them under her wing when they first started working for Zeke, when they were still new and terrified.

"I don't know. It's complicated. I don't know if it's even possible," Tao begins, then pauses. Thinks.

"Intriguing," Pru jumps in, and her eyes flit to Tao's face, at the tattoos that already litter it. "Not doubting my abilities, are you?"

Tao shakes their head.

"No, it's not that. It's just I've researched it a little and I can't find it online. It's still a protection spell, but I want—I don't know. Protection against myself? For other people? Is that a thing?"

Pru looks at Tao for a long time, something like steel in her gaze. She opens her mouth a couple of times to speak but seemingly thinks better of it.

"Why would you want that?" she asks finally.

"It's something I've been thinking about for a while," Tao lies. "You know, picking up more powers. I don't want to hurt anybody if I pick up the wrong one."

"The vast majority of powers are utterly benign unless you truly mean to harm someone," Pru points out, and it's true. But Tao can't tell her the truth. Not exactly.

"It's just my dreams. They've got me thinking. They end badly. For other people. And I know that might not mean anything, but I'm scared it might. The wrong bit of empathy on the wrong day at the wrong time. Who knows what's out there?" Tao says, and at this, Pru grins a little, that odd smirk that lights up her face.

"That is true," she says. "The world is stranger than we know. But you shouldn't be scared of the dreams. I don't think you're going to hurt anybody."

"I just don't even want it to be a possibility," Tao says, and Pru nods.

"Okay, my strange little sibling with so many secrets to keep. I'll tattoo you. I have some time. But you have to crush all my charcoal for me as payment. I hate doing it. Gets under my nails even when I wear gloves, and you know I hate wearing gloves." Her eyes drift down to Tao's gloved hands. "Not that you'd mind that, I suppose."

Tao resists the urge to clench their fingers and instead offers a small smile.

"Okay, deal," they say. "I'll crush your charcoal. I would have paid cash, but if you'd prefer."

"Oh, I do prefer," she says, and Tao can see her point. Crushing charcoal to add to the inks is slow, laborious work, and the dust and mess of it can get everywhere.

"Thank you," Tao says sincerely.

She yawns again, wide, and does actually cover her mouth when it goes on longer than she must have expected.

"You'll be turning up late next," Tao says, and she just looks at them sharply, like they've unwittingly said the wrong thing. There's the urge to apologize, but what for?

"Little sibling, I'd be early to my own funeral. Now, I have a client in about ten minutes, so this therapy session is over. Besides, Zeke is giving us one of his looks again."

Tao takes the hint and heads back over to their own station, but not before dragging the wheelie chair back to where it had been. They only have one client this morning, so they could step out and get coffee, but instead, they reach for their sketchbook.

They flip through the pages until they get to the drawing they're looking for—Adam's wolfsbane. Normally, once a tattoo has been claimed, it gets crossed out with thick black marker, but Tao finds they can't quite bring themself to do it. Instead they run a gloved finger over the gray pencil marks that make up the small flowers.

They had given Adam that protection, hadn't they? Would it still work even against themself?

They hoped never to find out. And besides, Pru would hopefully be able to—to what? To neuter Tao's power? Was that what they even wanted? Were they willing to give that up just for Adam?

Because it does feel like giving something up. Despite the utter taboo of it, it is a part of Tao.

And a part of someone else too. Someone else far more danger-ous than Tao.

If Tao puts a leash on their own abilities, what does that mean for their hopes of stopping the other necromancer? Was it even up to them to do so?

Tao stares at the bouquet of wolfsbane. No, this is the right choice. Somebody else would notice the missing person soon.

Tao couldn't be expected to fight a rogue necromancer.

As much as they despise the authorities, the censorship, the *shoot first, ask questions later* attitude, it was up to them. Not Tao.

If only Tao could bring themself to believe that.

Chapter Seven

Tao spends the morning with mortar and pestle in hand, painstakingly crushing charcoal for Pru, and the soot and ash residue get everywhere, as predicted. This particular charcoal is supposed to have burned under a full moon, and that's supposed to make all the difference, though really, Tao isn't so sure. Maybe it's simply a matter of intent and belief—if someone believes that adding this charcoal makes the inks more powerful, then it must be so.

Their arms are aching by lunchtime, several small bags of black powder successfully labeled and put aside, and they consider going to lunch, feeling the lack of their missed coffee that morning. Zeke and Pru are both busy tattooing, privacy charms up, so there's nothing to do but wait to ask. They could just leave, but something tells them to stay a little while longer.

As if wished into existence, not five minutes later, the door pushes open and Adam walks in. Tao does a small double take, not expecting to see him until later that evening, and Pru pauses her tattooing to turn in her chair and level a stare at Tao and raise her eyebrows inscrutably before going back to her work.

Tao stumbles to their feet and walks over to greet Adam, who holds a to-go coffee cup and a muffin in careful hands.

"What are you doing here?" Tao asks, and Adam smiles and blushes a little. "Is that hot chocolate?"

"Well, this is, in hindsight, really dumb, but I realized yesterday we didn't agree on a time and place to meet tonight, so I took my lunch break and thought, well, I could bring you lunch? And I saw you get the hot chocolate and muffin yesterday, and well, it made sense in my head," Adam rambles, half-broken sentences on nervous tongue.

"It's not dumb." Tao smiles and takes the still warm hot chocolate from Adam. They take. a sip. It's perfect. "I just hope you didn't have to come far. Look, come sit down. You can stay for a little while, right?"

"I can," Adam says. He follows Tao back to their workstation, hops up on the tattoo bench, and pats the leather beside them for Tao to join him. Tao can feel the eyes of Pru and Zeke on them both. They fish out their own privacy charm and place it next to them as they sit beside Adam.

"To answer your other question." Adam steals a small piece of Tao's muffin in a move Tao finds inexplicably adorable. "I haven't come far. I work at the library. The one in the old temple? I'm a junior archivist there. Mainly rare books. We have the largest collection of some types of texts this side of the continent."

Adam speaks with such enthusiasm his entire face lights up with it, making him seem younger. He's so bright, like sunshine. It almost hurts Tao to look at him. Tao focuses on their hot chocolate and not the way Adam's thigh is dangerously close to their own.

"You like it there," Tao says, and it's a statement, not a question. Adam smiles wider.

"I love it, which really surprised me. I dropped out of university and took the first internship I could find. I was lucky it was the library. They took me on, and it's just been brilliant. I've learned so much. Knowledge is power, right?"

Tao thinks back to the night before, when they searched and found nothing about a lack of powers in adults. Maybe that's why Adam is so in love with the library—it's a more unrestricted way of accessing knowledge. Maybe there are even books there that explain Adam to himself.

"I think power is power, generally speaking. But yeah, the argument for knowledge is becoming, I don't know…. I get what you mean. It must be nice. Quiet," Tao says.

"Yeah, we're a quiet bunch. Actually tangent, but I promise it's still related. Your tattoo—I'm not sure what to call them, tattoo guns?" Adam pauses and waits for Tao to correct him.

"Machines, tattoo machines. No guns here," Tao says, and Adam nods and steals another piece of muffin.

"Right, so your tattoo machines. They don't have to be as noisy as they are, right? They could be charmed quieter. Someone out there knows how to do that. So why don't they?" Adam asks. He shifts almost imperceptibly. His thigh brushes Tao's, denim to denim, and Tao is hit again with that *want-urge-need* of sensation. They swallow it down and try to ignore it. It's not as bad as yesterday, but it's still overwhelming. Their hand shakes as they take another sip of hot chocolate.

"Erm," they say, briefly forgetting what Adam was saying. "Oh, right. The tattoo machines. Well, it's the same as everything else, really. Sure, they're noisy and kind of scary, but that means they're working, right? They're seen to be working. And that increases the power of the tattoo, because it's—not an invasion, but it's, well, it's ritual, I suppose. The same reason we don't numb the skin. We could, but that pain, it lends credence to what's happening. People believe in it because it's seen as such a drastic intervention in their lives. And sometimes, that extra bit of belief can be hugely powerful."

"Feedback loops again." Adam looks down at the muffin he's been picking at. "Oh, I've basically finished this. I'm sorry. I'll get you another one."

"No, it's okay, stay. I wasn't that hungry. Plus you didn't get your hands on the hot chocolate." Tao smiles, and Adam beams back, impossible, vibrant, and so alive.

"I really am sorry all the same," Adam says.

"You're apologizing again. That seems to be all we do to each other. How about we don't from now on? Unless we really mean it?" Tao says, feeling strange that they've already built this small language between them, a little ritual of their own, just as real as any other.

"Okay, well, can I ask another question, then?" Adam says, and Tao nods around their hot chocolate. "So, you have a lot of tattoos. Obviously. But—why? Are they all protective? Wouldn't one work as well as dozens?"

Tao carefully puts the hot chocolate down and thinks for a few seconds before answering. They like Adam, really like him, more by the minute. There are boundaries, of course there are, but somehow they seem less important than they did before. All the rules are falling away, and the want echoing inside Tao now isn't just from their power but from their very soul. How could they throw away this boy who asks so many questions, who is so curious, who brings Tao hot chocolate and a muffin, even if he eats the muffin himself?

It's impossible. Tao shouldn't even consider this, shouldn't even be in this position. And yet, they are. And they're not sure they would want to change that.

"When I was a kid, we moved around a lot," Tao begins, scratching at old wounds now, scars they haven't opened in years. "My parents were always chasing... something. Something better—a better life, more money, more opportunities. I never felt like I had a home. It was more a place to stay before we started moving again. I don't think they wanted a kid, not really, but they had me, and I guess that really bothered them, because they treated me like I was some almighty burden, like somehow I was hindering them in all they wanted to achieve." Tao pauses and feels Adam's thigh against theirs again, more insistent now, and while their power screams at them, there's comfort there too. "We'd been in Nomos three months, and I'd just turned eighteen. And they decided I should strike out on my own. Just like they had. Gave me enough money for three months' rent and kicked me out. Told me not to come home. And so I didn't."

Adam breathes in a harsh breath. "I'm so sorry that happened to you."

Tao shakes their head. "It's okay. It's not your fault."

"No, but I can still be sorry. No kid should have to go through that."

The press of a thigh again.

"So I started applying for jobs, anything, because I couldn't let that money run out. I was so scared. I found this place, and it was like—for the first time it really felt like home. I wanted so badly to work here. I guess I practically begged Zeke in the end. And I guess he saw something in me he liked, because he took me on as an apprentice. And I've been here ever since.

"The tattoos are a reminder of that. I guess I need those reminders. Zeke did the first few, and Pru's done a few too. It reminds me that I'm loved. That I'm safe. Protected. And I guess I hope the tattoos will let me stay that way, that my life won't be uprooted again, that home stays home. Sorry." Tao wipes at their face, closing their eyes and trying to keep calm.

"Hey, it's all right." And then there's the pressure of an arm around their shoulders, and how their power leaps at that, practically frothing at the bit to *take take take*. And yet they don't. They don't want to. Instead, they lean into the touch and let Adam hold them.

"You got black on your face," Adam says after a minute, and Tao curses, remembering the charcoal. Adam laughs, small and barely there, but it's enough to draw a watery smile from Tao. "There, that's better. You look so good when you smile."

"Could say the same to you," Tao says, and Adam ducks his head. "I can't believe I never noticed you before. It's like you just started existing yesterday. How is that possible?"

"Maybe there's a book at the library for that," Adam says, and maybe, Tao thinks, there is.

"Excuse me," comes a voice, and Tao and Adam look away from each other to see Zeke standing just outside the privacy charm. Zeke is smiling indulgently. "This is a place of business."

Tao pockets the privacy charm and lets the spell drop, and Adam slides down from the tattoo bench and holds Tao's arm as they follow. When their feet hit the floor, it's like something has changed. Nothing they could put their finger on, but it's different nonetheless.

"If you could, I'd be delighted to see the work Tao did on you yesterday, kid," Zeke says, and Adam glances at Tao and then rolls up his sleeve. The wolfsbane tattoo stands proud, less red than yesterday, the black lines still slightly raised but no longer angry-looking.

Zeke takes gentle hold of Adam's hand to rotate his wrist back and forth as he looks at the tattoo.

"It's good work," Zeke says after a minute. "Solid. It'll hold. It's already doing its job. You must come back sometime. I'm sure Tao would be delighted to tattoo you again."

"We could give you the family discount!" Pru calls from across the shop, and Tao feels their cheeks flush.

"Ignore her," Zeke says. "But do return. It is good to see a friendly face. I do think we'll be seeing a lot of you."

"I hope so, sir." Adam smiles, and Zeke drops his wrist. Adam doesn't roll down his sleeve, instead letting the tattoo be visible a moment longer.

"Now make your plans and shoo. Tao cannot sit around all day wooing young men. This is not that sort of establishment," Zeke says, smile hiding behind his eyes, knowing he's embarrassing Tao.

"Sorry, sir," Adam says, though he doesn't sound it. It's nice to watch, Tao thinks, Zeke and Adam getting on. Anything else would be awful.

"None of the 'sir' business, please. And I'm sure Tao will tell you I'm more easily won over with baked goods." Zeke smiles, wider this time, and then retreats.

"So, I should definitely go." Adam nudges Tao's arm with his own. All this touching is knotting Tao's stomach in the strangest way, their power confused. If it's not supposed to take from this boy, what is it supposed to do? Tao isn't sure.

"Yeah, sorry about Zeke. And Pru," Tao says.

"They're okay. I like them. So... I'll meet you. What time do you finish here?" Adam asks.

"Five, round about."

"Okay, so if I meet you at five thirty outside the coffee shop?" Adam says, and Tao nods.

"What are we going to do?" Tao asks, and Adam smiles that sunshine smile.

"That's for me to know and you to find out," he says, and before Tao can stop him, he reaches out to trace the line of tattoos from Tao's hairline to their jaw. The touch is incredible, unbelievable. Whatever an act of violence is, it's the ultimate opposite. Tao leans into it, and their power is silent, watching, waiting, observing.

"This is a place of business!" Zeke calls from across the shop, and they spring apart.

"Okay. I really am going to go now. I don't want to annoy your boss," Adam says and reluctantly steps away. Tao feels the loss immediately.

"I'll see you tonight," Tao says, already counting down the seconds.

"Yeah," Adam says softly and then starts to walk away. He pauses at the door, looks back, and smiles again. Impossible smiles.

And then he's gone, swallowed by the city.

Tao's power rumbles beneath their skin. The world has shifted slightly on its axis.

Adam makes them want to forget everything that isn't Adam-related. And yet, at the same time, Adam drew out the worst of Tao's childhood, a story that took Zeke months. Even Pru doesn't know it all, not really. The only other person in this world who does, aside from Tao's parents—and could they ever understand what damage they caused?—is Luis.

"He still gives me weird vibes," Pru says, brushing past Tao to get to the back room.

Me too, me too.

CHAPTER EIGHT

ZEKE HAD stepped out, drawn by the promise of the baked goods and coffee across the street, and there didn't seem a more perfect time for Pru to tattoo Tao than then.

"Are you ready, little sibling?" Tao looks up, and Pru is smiling crookedly down at them, hands on her hips. She still looks tired, more so even than this morning, which makes sense, but the dark circles under her eyes stand out against her dark eyeliner.

"Ready," Tao says.

They head over to Pru's workstation, and Tao hops up onto the leather bench.

"Where do you want it?" Pru asks, and Tao places a finger on a small gap of skin between their ear and cheek. There's just enough space for something small, something that, despite seeing Adam earlier and the way their power seemed to quiet, still feels essential.

Pru disinfects the area, grabs a Sharpie, and starts drawing, brow furrowed in concentration. It's the work of a few strokes, and Tao tries to decipher them from the sensation alone. Soon Pru pulls back and reaches behind her to grab a mirror.

There's a simple tilted circle design, a cross positioned halfway through it, in keeping with the rest of Tao's tattoos.

"I've never done anything like this before," Pru says honestly. "But that doesn't mean I can't."

She snaps on gloves and checks her machine. It buzzes loud and clear.

"You using that charcoal I oh-so-painstakingly crushed for you this morning?" Tao asks, and Pru pokes their cheek.

"Quiet, you. Can't have you distracting me now," Pru says. "Ready?"

Tao nods. Pru lowers the tattoo machine, and Tao closes their eyes, instinct, the needle too close for comfort. Pru would never, ever harm them, but there's something primal about it nonetheless.

"Here we go." Pru etches in the first line.

It feels wrong immediately.

Tao's skin burns where the ink is settling. It's not the normal, almost pleasant sting of a fresh tattoo, but hot-cold fire spreading outward, and they daren't move, not with that buzzing needle so close to their eye, but they must make a sound, because Pru pauses for a moment.

"Okay?" She sounds concerned.

The pain doesn't recede, and Tao wonders if this is the cost of locking away the power they were born with. It makes sense. Of course it was going to hurt. They nod, despite all their instincts.

The needle hits skin again, another dragging line, and Tao's muscles clench and then start to shake. Something's really wrong. Behind their eyelids they can see sparks—little white explosions—and when they open their eyes, the world is grayer than it should be, fuzzy and blackening around the edges. They can't stop shaking, and the burning is spreading, encompassing the entire side of their face now, spreading down past their jaw and toward their spine.

They can't hear properly, can't make out what Pru's saying, only the worry in her voice carrying across the shop and then, a few seconds later, the gravel of Zeke's voice. A steady hand rests on Tao's shoulder, grounding, and Tao shudders against it, feeling sick, feeling like they might die, and their power leaps and laps at the contact, trying to save itself, trying to fight off what's happening to it, to Tao.

Zeke speaks, and Tao's body goes limp. They close their eyes again, the black becoming too much, and lie heavy and broken on the tattoo bench.

"I—don't know what happened." Pru's voice filters through.

Zeke says something Tao can't make out, and there's movement beside them. The machine buzzes again. *No, no more.*

"Not pretty," Zeke growls, and then the needle is hitting skin again, and Tao's skin aches with it, tries to pull at the brief contact of fingers that hold the skin taut and keep their head steady.

It seems to last years, decades. A millennium could pass, and the burning is spreading down Tao's spine and to their limbs. Unable to move, unable to scream or even cry, Tao lies there and focuses on the lines of the needle as they spread farther onto Tao's cheek, and then round back toward their ear. It feels huge. It feels like—like if they ever open their eyes again, the entire side of their face will be blacked out, a thousand symbols etched in, each one of them a violation, pain and fire and a sense of dread that Tao can't shake.

Tao tries to think of Adam, the promise of Adam, meeting Adam at the coffee shop and the safety they'd felt in Adam's arms, telling Adam secrets and trusting that he'd keep them safe. Doing this to keep Adam safe, this huge and terrible thing that is clenching their organs and making their heart beat so fast now it feels like it might just explode.

Sweat dries cold on Tao's skin, and they want to shiver but still can't move. They can't do anything. They're helpless, utterly help-less, and whatever is happening now, there's no control there, and it's terrifying.

The needle moves close to their eye socket and vibrates against bone, and they wish they could flinch away. *It's too much. Let it end. Let it be over. Let it stop.*

The last few lines, though Tao doesn't know that they are the last, seem to take a lifetime, but with each one that settles beneath skin, their body begins to calm and the fire in their veins starts to recede. Their heart slows, and their guts unclench. They open their eyes, catch the glare of a head torch, and wince. But it's Zeke—Zeke staring down at them, Zeke's worried expression, and Zeke's fingers pressed to Tao's temple. Zeke's magic holding Tao's body still so he can work.

The buzz of the machine stops, and sensation returns to Tao's limbs like a rush of cold water flowing through their body from head to toe.

They try to sit up, but someone—Zeke?—holds them down. Someone else, it must be Pru, places a hand on their calf and strokes small circles there, calming, though Tao can hear more clearly now, and Pru's breathing is ragged, like she's been crying.

"What—what happened?" Tao stutters out, tongue feeling too heavy in their mouth, hitting their teeth all wrong.

Pru starts to cry again, muffled little sobs. Zeke sighs, and Tao looks at him, watching as he switches off the headlamp and removes it, placing it to one side so that Tao can see him clearly. For the first time in all the years Tao's known him, he doesn't look ageless, he looks impossibly old.

"I screwed up!" Pru exclaims, and Zeke's face doesn't change, except for a small flicker that's gone so quickly Tao could have imagined it.

"Conflict," Zeke says after a moment of careful thought. "Something akin to an immune response. Your body rejected the tattoo utterly, nearly killing you in the process. Foolish, all of it."

"I'm sorry," Pru says, sounding utterly distraught. "I didn't know that could happen!"

Zeke rounds on her, face no longer calm. "Then why do it, then? Why attempt such a thing? Why would you not come to me first? Do you trust me that little? Or do you think so highly of yourself that you thought it unnecessary to do so?"

Pru recoils, and Tao wants to too. They close their eyes again, but soon Zeke is speaking again, demanding their full attention.

"To try to negate a power is like committing heresy. It is like removing a limb and expecting it not to bleed. You tried to rip it out, but you could never have succeeded. It would have died with Tao before allowing itself to be destroyed," Zeke says, spitting angry in a way Tao has never seen him. It's a protective anger, justified, but still, Tao feels awful for Pru.

"I asked for it," Tao says, words coming more easily now. "I asked Pru to do it."

"You didn't know what you were asking for, and neither did she. Why you would do this I cannot begin to comprehend. I thought I had taught you both better than this."

"Tao asked for a protection charm. That's all it was. To protect other people from themselves. We do protection charms all the time. That's what this shop *is*!" Pru says, trying to make sense of it as she speaks.

"Conflict!" Zeke exclaims, louder now, and Tao jumps slightly. "There is conflict in what you're trying to accomplish. Tao's powers, and I cannot tell you what they may be because I do not know and Tao is under no obligation to tell me, are at odds with what they asked you to do. Not because they would ever harm someone, but because some part of their power is innately destructive. And I trust that Tao will never use that to harm someone, may not even have been aware that it was so, but nevertheless, when it saw it was threatened, it reacted as readily as any cornered animal. And you nearly killed your *little sibling*." Zeke spits the words.

"I'm sorry!" Pru begs. "I'm so sorry." She pauses. "I'm sorry, Tao."

"It's okay," Tao says, because it's not her fault. She doesn't know the half of it. This power, this necromancy, hidden and taboo and unexplained? How could she have known? There is such potential for harm. Tao's dreams bear that out, and so does the necromancer still at large. It's a dangerous power, and there is no peaceful way to use it. Tao thinks about the way it tries to latch on to Adam, and gods—Adam—this was all for him, and now Tao knows Adam will never be entirely safe around them.

"But your face, oh gods, your face," Pru says, and Tao makes to lift a hand to where their cheek stings with the memory of the needle. "Zeke, show them. I can't."

Zeke helps Tao sit up, adjusting the bench so they can still lean back. He hands Tao the mirror, and for a moment, Tao dare not look. They bring it up to their face, not knowing what to expect.

The entirety of their cheek up to their eye on the left side of their face is covered in hastily tattooed marks. Not the elegant marks that decorate the rest of their face, but ugly, defensive marks that surround and protect against the original tattoo—Pru's tattoo—which is now an ugly brand, welted red and raised. Their face barely looks like their face anymore, so changed by the ink. It's hard to process, no matter how long Tao stares.

"I'm sorry," Pru says again.

"You were bleeding out. I had to cauterize the wound," Zeke says, and the metaphor makes sense. It's ugly, but it's done the job.

"I was supposed to meet Adam tonight," Tao says, more to themself than anybody else.

"You can!" Pru says. "You should."

Tao looks to Zeke, not trusting Pru's judgment right now.

"I agree, actually. This has been—unfortunate. But do not let it be the thing that defines today. You will grow used to what has been done to you, though I know it is the utmost violation. I believe, though, that your Adam will not think any less of you for what you look like, for what it's worth. There is no way to ask for forgiveness for these actions, however necessary they may have been. Know that I saved your life, but I did so at a cost. And that cost was the removal of your autonomy, that I violated your consent in a way that is unconscionable. And I will live with that, have to live with that, for a long time, and so will Pru. And unfortunately, so will you. But know this—the marks you wear now are marks of survival. And hopefully, a lesson learned, though one I wish I could have prevented. Go home, change, and meet your boy. There is still good in this world, in this day. Tell him what you must, and try to be honest, if you can. Own these mistakes, else they shall own you. I need to talk to Prudence alone now, so go. And I am sorry too. I hope you know that."

Tao can feel their heart breaking for Zeke with every word. It's not his fault. It's Tao's fault, Pru's fault, perhaps. Maybe nobody's. A decision made without any realization of the potential consequences.

"It's okay," Tao says and means it. They stand slowly, expecting their legs to feel shaky but instead find strength there. "You saved me. I owe you so much for that."

"Do not attempt this again." Zeke pats Tao's shoulder. Tao's power rises and falls at the touch. "Though I feel I can leave that unsaid."

"I won't," Tao says and turns to look at Pru. "I'm so sorry for asking you to do this, Pru. I should have realized."

She launches herself at them in a rib-cracking hug.

"Get home safe, okay?" she says into their ear. They nod. Slowly, she releases them. "It kind of suits you, actually," she says, looking at Tao's face. Then she shakes her head. "Sorry, I shouldn't have said that."

"Too soon, perhaps," Zeke agrees, "but she is not wrong. You bear marks of power and protection stronger than you ever did previously. Marks of a survivor. Try to find pride in them."

Tao nods and swallows hard, feeling emotional. Their friends, flawed, imperfect, but still so full of love.

"I'll see you Monday, then." Tao gives a small cautious wave and leaves the shop. They start walking. They reach the second corner before they start to cry.

CHAPTER NINE

TAO STEPS into the shower without even looking into the bathroom mirror. They know their eyes must be puffy and red and that their tattoos will be similar, and there's nothing they can do about either of those things.

They run the water hot, as though it'll wash away all things, some kind of absolution, as though the mistakes of the day can be cleansed through reddened skin and a cloud of steam.

They feel exhausted, and as they raise their face to the water, it stings, and they can almost imagine all that ink running right off them and down the drain. But it's never that easy.

Finally, because they don't want to be late for Adam, who would probably be far too patient for far too long and not even want to hear their apologies, they step out and, with a damp hand, wipe the mirror clear.

A face that both is their face and isn't stares back at them. The shower has cleaned away the spare smudges of ink, leaving the lines more defined now, raised and sore but less violent than they looked in the studio. Except for that initial mark, Pru's mark—which looks more like a brand than a tattoo now, raised angrily against their skin, the ink almost gone entirely, just sore, red, and likely to puff up and scar.

The tattoos that counter it surround it like soldiers in position, echoing out across Tao's skin. It makes sense now in a way it didn't before—how many and how much—that a countercharm must always be more aggressive than what it is countering, for any charm that is stanching metaphorical bleeding also points out the fact that said bleeding is occurring.

Feedback loops.

Tao isn't sure what they'll tell Adam. Perhaps some vague version of the truth. It doesn't matter, they decide, because after tonight, they won't be seeing Adam again. It's too dangerous, and today has proven that.

Hasn't it?

True, Adam brought them hot chocolate and touched them, and their power had initially reared up, only to be tamed and confused by the sensation. It was… nice. What a small word to describe something so impossible, something Tao has spent their entire life avoiding. But it suits. Adam is nice, and being touched by Adam is nice, and Tao wants more of that and can't have it.

But they have tonight. Like some kind of crooked compromise, they have tonight, and for this night alone, they can pretend they're normal, can pretend like there's no time limit, that their power isn't so immensely dangerous that it nearly killed them.

Gods, Tao nearly died. Would have died if Zeke hadn't known what to do. The urge to cry rises up again, but Tao shoves it down. They stare at their face, and their face stares back.

This is my face now. And then they turn away from the mirror to get dressed.

They hadn't thought about what they were going to wear, because they would have been coming straight from the shop, which, with ink splashes and spills, requires dark clothing, but now everything has changed and they have to make decisions.

They rifle through their wardrobe for something that, oh, that Adam would like. They pull out a button-down shirt and then discard it. As tempting as it is to dress up, to play a role, Adam knows them as someone who wears a hoodie and jeans, so that's who they'll be. It was enough before; it should be enough now.

Still, they pull out the hoodie with the fewest holes.

And their best jeans.

They glance at their phone to check the time and then decide to braid their hair. They can do it if they're quick. So they separate it into chunks and weave in intricate patterns, until one central braid falls from their forehead down their back and two more on either side pull tight to the side of their head. They add a couple of protective trinkets Pru had given them—tiny stones on gold rings that loop through the hair—and then they're done. Maybe, in some small way, it's an attempt at distraction. It's hard to say.

They need to leave, need to get to the coffee shop. Their heartbeat quickens at the thought of Adam waiting there.

They grab their gloves and pull them on with the practiced ease of muscle memory, and then their coat, and head out the door with their phone clenched in their hand and their keys in their teeth. They try not to slam the door, but nevertheless it bangs shut, and that summons Luis, who must wait by the doormat to scold them.

"Terrible child!" Luis exclaims as he pulls his door open. Then he pauses. "Oh, what have you done to your face?" Luis's own face pulls together in concern. Tao raises a hand to their cheek and then drops it down to their side again.

"There was an accident. It's okay, Luis," they say, trying for reassuring. Luis doesn't look like he believes them, but lets it go.

"Well, don't forget, tomorrow—Spaghetti Saturday! The most important day of the week! I expect to see you there!" Luis crows, and Tao smiles despite themself.

"Of course," they say.

"Now go! What are you doing talking to me, terrible child? You obviously have places to be! Go, go, go!" Luis shoos, so Tao takes the hint and goes, taking the steps two at a time as usual, anxiety and anticipation muddling in their veins and turning their thoughts to mush.

They purposefully avoid the alleyway, opting for the longer route. After tonight, after Adam, after all of that, they'll focus on the other necromancer. Somehow they'll find them and stop them. They try not to think about how negligent they've been in not acting, but… they're afraid.

The other necromancer has power, and Tao doesn't know how much. Enough, certainly, and every time they kill, they will only amass more. Just because Tao only knows of one body doesn't mean there *is* only one.

Why hasn't anybody noticed? Or have they? Are the police, or perhaps some government body higher still than that, searching right now? Are their guns ready, are their nerves as frayed as Tao's as they hunt down whoever is doing this?

And will Tao get caught in the crossfire of it all? Will the dreams bear it out? Will it all come down to mud and dirt and—

Adam. Adam was there the last time.

Tao knows then that tonight can only ever be tonight, that Adam can't be allowed to stay in their life. Even putting aside their own power, Tao is in the line of sight of a necromancer, an honest-to-gods necromancer, and has been for months now if the dreams are any indication. They can't just ignore that and drag Adam into it.

They can only hope it isn't already too late.

They reach the coffee shop at a couple of minutes past five and slip inside, wondering if Adam will be taking them to eat or not. Either way, they're starving and could definitely eat again, so they order a muffin and a coffee and sit in a corner seat to watch the door. The coffee warms them and drives away the worst of the fatigue, and with every passing minute, their heart leaps a little more every time the door swings open to reveal someone new.

They manage to eat the muffin even as their nerves continue to build, though it tastes like nothing with every bite. They keep checking their phone for the time, tapping it awake and then watching the screen turn black again.

At exactly half past, the door opens and it's Adam—Adam after a long day of work, hair ruffled and glasses farther down his nose now, revealing the expanse of freckles there. Adam whose eyes are still so dark, like Tao could fall right into them and spend forever climbing out. Adam who scans the shop and lights up when he sees Tao, then makes his way over, chin buried in a tartan scarf and body swamped by his thick coat.

He's important, Tao thinks, and that's why he has to be protected.

"You're here!" Adam exclaims as he drops into the seat beside Tao's. His cheeks are a little flushed and drawn chubby by the smile that stretches across his face.

"I'm here." Tao waits as Adam looks at them, watching his eyes for the moment he really notices the new tattoos. Waiting for—some kind of rejection. Perhaps that'd be easier.

"You got some new—" Adam gestures to where the marks would be on his own face. His smile doesn't dip or change. He just seems intrigued. "They look sore," he continues, and that is tinged with something else. Concern?

"Is it okay if we don't talk about it?" Tao asks. "Just for tonight?" *We only have tonight*, they don't say.

"Of course, yeah. I'm sorry, yeah. I didn't realize. So, I'm glad you got coffee, because I realized I totally hadn't planned anywhere for us to eat. It's not that kind of—gods, am I allowed to call this a date? Are you okay with that? Because it doesn't have to be." Adam rambles, and it's delightful, and it warms something inside Tao that has long since burned out.

"We can call it a date." They smile, real and true. They forget for a moment that this can't last, that this is a one-time deal. They decide to forget. Just one night. One brilliant night and then they'll remind themself.

"I'm glad," Adam says. "I was really worried. I couldn't remember what I'd said. I thought, well, maybe you'd just want to be friends, and maybe you'll still think that after tonight. I don't know. But I really—is it daft that I really like you? I barely know you and I really like you. And I keep telling myself how silly that sounds, but I do, and I can't turn it off. I don't want to turn it off. So here I am. And I'm probably freaking you out right now." Adam chews nervously on his bottom lip.

"You're not. I promise. I like you too. Perhaps more than I should," Tao admits. A small truth.

"Oh, okay. I mean, good. But—more than you should? That sounds ominous. Don't—I don't know, don't think you can't like me as much as you want. Gods know I do. Like you, not me. More than I should." Adam stumbles over his words, and it's too endearing. And Tao does like him so much more than they should, more by the minute, the words piling up and etching themselves onto Tao's bones, where they'll echo forever, long after tonight.

"Do you want anything? Coffee?" Tao asks, and the mood bends but doesn't break.

"No, I got some at work. Terrible stuff, but it does the trick. You can probably tell." Adam smiles again admitting this. "I was a bit nervous, and it hasn't helped."

"I was nervous too," Tao says, feeling raw and honest and like they would tell Adam anything if he only asked.

"Don't be nervous," Adam says, as though it's that simple. Perhaps it can be, for one night.

"Okay," Tao says.

"Just like that?" Adam grins impossibly wide. He could power a sun with that grin, bring light to an entire solar system.

"Just like that," Tao confirms as they reach across to where Adam's arm rests on his knee. It's a small touch, barely there, a kind of test. Tao's power uncurls and stretches like a sleeping cat, but doesn't reach out for Adam. It just waits, like it's looking to Tao to tell it what to do.

"Well, I can't argue with that," Adam says, looking at where Tao's hand had touched the fabric of his coat. "Should we be going, then?"

"Where are we going?" Tao asks, and Adam laughs a little.

"You'll think this is so daft, but back to the library, actually. I wanted to show you something that mattered to me. I couldn't think of it, but then it hit me. The most precious thing I've found in the years I've worked there. Possibly the most precious set of books in the world. A lifetime, written in ink. I thought to myself, this is it, isn't it? This is what I want to show Tao. This beautiful, rare thing. Because that's what you are. A beautiful, rare thing." Adam blushes deep red at that and won't meet Tao's eyes, until suddenly he does, and Tao knows they were right about how they could fall right in, and gods, how they want to.

They don't even try to argue with what Adam said. They just sit in the warm glow of it, unable to move, glad to be alive, glad to be sitting with a beautiful boy who is so generous with his words.

"What book is it?" Tao asks eventually, after what feels like forever has passed while the two of them stare at one another.

"I want to introduce you to the diaries of Mary Mallon. The most famous necromancer nobody's ever heard of," Adam says, and there's no fear in his words.

Tao's stomach drops, their mouth suddenly dry.

"You're not afraid of necromancers, are you?" Adam asks.

CHAPTER TEN

TAO DOESN'T know what to say or if there are even words. They feel like they're floating above themself, looking down, waiting for an answer just as much as Adam is.

"Sorry," Adam says, interrupting their thoughts. "Wow, I—I forget sometimes that it's actually a big deal. People take it all really seriously. And you know, quite right too, but it's fascinating, isn't it?"

"Can we talk about this somewhere else?" Tao asks, aware that anybody could be listening.

"Yeah, sure." Adam holds out a hand to help Tao up. This time, Tao takes it, and their power writhes and pokes, confused, but they're beginning to understand it a little now. It's trying to figure out if Adam is a threat. As much as the protective charms tattooed into their skin, Tao's power is a defense against the outside world—an awful, all-destructive defense, but a defense nonetheless. Tao tries to calm themself, and their power rests again, allowing them to savor the firm grasp of Adam's hand on theirs.

Soon they're both outside of the coffee shop, the cold evening air brisk on their cheeks, flushing their noses red.

"I understand, you know," Adam says when the crowd thins and it's just the two of them on the sidewalk. "Not wanting to talk in public. I forget how taboo it is sometimes. That's on me, for sure. I sort of—I live those diaries, you know? I've read them more times than I could count. And if I've learned anything, it's that I can't be scared of born necromancers."

You should be scared; you should be so scared.

And then their brain catches up to what Adam said. *Born necromancers.* They haven't heard of that before. It must show in their face, because Adam smiles and starts to talk again.

"A born necromancer is someone born with that power. And almost one hundred percent of the time, they'll live their entire lives without harming anyone. We don't even know how many of them there have been, because they normally keep to themselves so much. We only know about Mary Mallon because of her journals, and that's only good luck and good record keeping."

"But there are other necromancers," Tao says, because they know that. They know there's one here, somewhere, in the city, in Nomos, and Adam should be scared.

"Yeah," Adam says nonchalantly, like he's discussing breakfast options or something. "Blood necromancers. Necromancy isn't passed on through empathy like other powers are, but by blood spilled. I don't know why—Mary Mallon had some ideas, but nothing concrete. You have to remember that this was the early twentieth century. She didn't have access to what we know now, which admittedly is still not a lot. A lot of information is still suppressed by the government. There's no way to search for it online, and the books we have on it aren't available to the public. I'm not even sure we're supposed to have them at all. But, you know, libraries. One of the first lines of defense against fascism and all that it entails."

It's a lot to take in very quickly. They both walk in silence for a few minutes.

"You think—you think stopping necromancers is fascist?" Tao asks after what seems like an age. It's a complicated sentence on their tongue, and one that sounds wrong even as they say it.

"I think the way the authorities, the police, go about it is, certainly. No born power should ever carry a death sentence. In the past it was lynch mobs, now it's a bullet to the brain. There's a distinction, of course, to be made between born and blood necromancers and the harm they do, but either way, the concept of an eye for an eye is dangerous. And not allowing people access to information that could potentially *prevent* the transmission of necromancy from a born necromancer to a potential blood necromancer? That's how you get those spikes, the outbreaks you see every so often. If people understood what they were doing, if they had the information, it might save a lot of lives." Adam talks with a certainty Tao hasn't heard from him before, the stuttered sentences gone now. Tao can tell he's in his element, that this is truly what he loves to talk about. But they can't understand why, of all things.

"So if you spill a born necromancer's blood, you become one?"

Tao asks, brain flicking back through their entire life, trying to think of moments when their own blood could have been spilled, when this power could have been spread. It's a harrowing thought and one they'll certainly dwell on. All the times they've been to the doctor, received vaccinations, gone to the dentist, does that count? They've never been in a fight, so are they safe? Have they infected anyone else? They can't have, surely. They'd have heard about it. It would have been traced back to them. But still, but still....

They walk past a park, dark green in the gathering moonlight. The old swing set, a faded red, squeaks gently in the wind.

"The library's not far now," Adam says. "But yes, if you spill a born necromancer's blood, you become one. And because of the nature of blood magic, it's a fast and brutal transfer of power and one that so often leads to the outbreaks of necromancy you see after a born necromancer has been attacked and driven out or killed." Adam says the last word strangely.

"Contagion," Tao says, mostly to themself.

"Essentially, yes. Imagine if one day you just picked up a brand-new power, fully formed, without that slow drip of empathy feeding it to you. I'd imagine it'd be all-encompassing. Dangerous. Heady. You'd want to see what you could do with it. And that always ends badly."

They pass a high set of railings, wrought iron and set into concrete high above the sidewalk, barring entry into the lush gardens beyond. Tao can spot well-maintained shrubbery and more than a few poisonous plants among the foliage.

They reach a gate, and Adam spreads his arms. For the first time, Tao really sees the building in front of them.

"Welcome to the Nomos Temple Public Library, my home away from home. And the home of Mary Mallon, possibly one of my favorite people ever."

It's an old temple, and the building reflects that in every way. Its high spires reach for the clouds. Stained-glass windows are dark now but must be colorful as rainbows during the day. There's an air of solidity to the building, like it has weathered many storms and will weather many more. It must have been here for centuries. Strangely, it reminds Tao of the tattoo studio. It emanates a kind of safety, and Tao can easily imagine why this was once a place of sanctuary.

"It's beautiful," Tao says, and Adam smiles wide.

"That it is," he says, and his nerves seem to have vanished now, his speech clearer and bolder. He's home, Tao realizes suddenly. This is where he feels safest.

Among books written by necromancers.

Adam fishes in his pocket for a small key and approaches the huge temple doors. It seems like far too small a key for such a building, but nonetheless, Adam fits it into a tiny, nearly impossible-to-find slot, and the doors creak their admittance.

"Perk of working here, I guess the ultimate perk, is coming here after hours. There's nothing I can do to harm the books. You'll see once we're inside, they're all protected from damage and from theft. They have more protective charms on them than you do," Adam says and smiles at Tao. Tao raises a hand instinctively to the new tattoos on their face, and Adam's smile falls a little. "It bothers you, doesn't it?" he asks. "You didn't choose it."

"No, I didn't," Tao says and leaves it at that. Adam nods and doesn't pursue the subject. Instead he tugs open one of the doors.

The library is massive, bigger even than it seems from the outside, and it feels sacred. Tao can feel the echoes of a thousand muttered prayers, of centuries of worship. And now the walls are lined with books, carefully arranged, not even remotely filling the space. In the center of the main room are long wooden tables, and even the tables look ancient, all knotted wood and woodworm, spread out with comfortable chairs tucked in beneath them.

The ceiling is several stories above and decorated with an intricate, impossible-to-decipher mural. The entire place is lit with charms, and amber light fills the space like the flames of an old fireplace. It even flickers a little.

"I know," Adam says. "It's pretty incredible. I can't believe I get to work here."

"It's safe," Tao says, not knowing what else to say. It feels like nothing could harm them here.

"It has been for a long time," Adam replies simply. "It's what it was built for. And it still serves its purpose to this day."

Adam points to a noticeboard, and Tao scans the bulletins, not

really knowing what they're looking at until they see it.
THE AUTHORITIES HAVE NOT BEEN HERE.
(WATCH VERY CLOSELY FOR THE REMOVAL
OF THIS SIGN.)

"One of the first lines of defense," Adam points out, as soon as he sees that Tao has spotted it. "We're not allowed to say that the authorities have been here, but we're allowed to say they haven't. And should that sign get removed at any point, well...." He shrugs.

"You really care," Tao says, "about what you're doing here."

"Knowledge is power, right? And people have the right to that knowledge and the right not to be surveilled while seeking it out. You'll see what I mean. Come on, I want to introduce you to Mary. She's a very special lady."

Adam leads Tao past the tables to a side room that looks ordinary until they step inside. It's an archive, a huge room full of more shelves and boxes. There's history in this room, history that has been forbidden and locked away for so long.

Adam walks through the stacks knowing exactly where he's headed. Tao follows, uncertain that they want to. They've never sought out information about necromancers, born or otherwise. It's always been too dangerous. And yet here Adam is, offering it to them, a smile on his face, eager, even.

"You're really not afraid of necromancers?" Tao can't help but ask. Adam swivels on his heel to turn to Tao and shrugs again.

"Not born necromancers, no. I think they were dealt a bad hand. It's a fluke of birth, power, and they happened to get one that society deems illegal. That's not their fault. They didn't ask for it. And like I said, the majority of them never even use it. It's the people who try to harm them that are dangerous."

"You sympathize with them, then?" Tao pushes, keeps pushing.

"I guess? Yeah. I do. I think, gods, imagine living your entire life knowing that if you slipped up, people would want to kill you. You've never done anything wrong, but your mere existence is enough to sentence you to death. Not that it'd work, of course."

"What do you mean? Why wouldn't it work? They kill necromancers all the time," Tao asks, confused. Adam turns and starts walking again but then pauses when he finds what he's looking for.

"Ah, here she is. The lady herself." He pulls out a small, ordinary-looking cardboard box. It looks so innocent, like there's no way it could blow Tao's world apart. The anxiety they've been feeling since Adam first asked them if they were scared of necromancers skyrockets.

Adam shuffles through the books, and they're fragile, delicate to Tao's eyes, but Adam doesn't treat them with any more care than any other book. He sees Tao looking.

"Protective charms, you have no idea. These babies survived the fire that killed Mary Mallon herself."

"So she's dead?" Tao asks.

"Well, that's the question of the hour, isn't it? Here. Listen to what she wrote about killing born necromancers," Adam says as he flicks to a page with well-practiced ease, like he's read it a hundred times before. Maybe he has. "'No weapon forged by man can kill a born necromancer.' That's what she says."

"What does that mean?" Tao asks, picturing police with guns and the indiscriminate use of force. Over and over again.

"Guns, knives, ropes, even fire, if it's man-made, won't kill a born necromancer. They're of the earth, you see? It's deep magic, rooted in the soil. Blood necromancy is—a pastiche, which is why they have to kill to continue to gain and use power. But a born necromancer? They draw it without even realizing, from the air, from the earth, from the people around them. Not enough to ever do any damage, but enough that they can be extraordinarily long-lived and can survive anything man can throw at them. They have to be killed by natural means." Adam pauses and pats the book in his hand. "Mary died in a fire. Probably. An accident. Her books survived because of their protective charms. They were discovered, and I've tried to trace this but I just can't find anything that links it together, but they ended up here. I don't know who knows we've got them, if anybody. I only found them by accident."

"Probably?" Tao asks, because Adam didn't sound at all sure that Mary was really dead.

"Well, I mentioned born necromancers were long-lived. How better to avoid suspicion than to fake your own death?" Adam muses. "No, I mean, fire isn't man-made. Unless, of course, she set it herself."

"You think about this a lot," Tao says.

"I think there's a lot to learn from Mary. I think if more people read her writing, we'd be able to completely reform how we treat born necromancers. You know she only raised one person in her life and that was an accident?"

"Who?" Tao asks, heart in their throat.

"Her five-year-old daughter." Adam smiles sadly. "She died so suddenly, and in her grief, Mary brought her back. But it wasn't her, was it? It never is. So despite all that grief, Mary wasn't blinded to what she had done. She laid her daughter back to the earth."

Tao thinks about the body in the alleyway, where it could be now. Will it get to be laid down again? Will Tao be the one to do it? Do they even have it within them to do so?

"This is a weird date, isn't it?" Adam says and shakes his head. "Sorry. I forget not everyone has the same views on necromancers as I do. I know it's considered taboo. I just—I wanted to share the most precious thing I had with you. I hope you don't—I hope you don't think it's too weird. I can trust you won't tell anyone about this, right?" The nerves have crept back in now, the delays between words and the stumbling sentences.

"You can trust me," Tao says and means it. "And—I wouldn't have chosen this, but that doesn't mean it was bad."

Adam puts the book down carefully on the shelf and moves a little closer to Tao, eyes scanning Tao's face.

"I think I would give you the world, and I barely even know you." Adam runs his hand down the side of Tao's face, careful to avoid those raw new tattoos. He pauses at Tao's chin, cups it with his hand, and draws Tao closer still.

They share the same air, breathing in and out in sync.

And then Adam leans in and kisses Tao.

CHAPTER ELEVEN

TAO KISSES back like it's the only thing they know how to do. Perhaps in that moment, it is.

Adam nudges in closer, skims his hands down the planes of Tao's cheeks, and cups their face like it's something precious. Tao's hands find Adam's waist, and their power *thrums*, alive and ready to strike if so commanded. Everything feels amplified—the way Adam's lips feel against theirs, the insistent push that opens to a gasp of a tongue flicking out—and isn't that something?

It's everything, everything, *everything*, and Tao has fallen and is falling, and it's not enough, never enough. It's all-encompassing and all they could ever want.

Adam nips gently at Tao's bottom lip and then pulls back.

They stare at each other for a moment, breathless, heady, mussed, and uncertain of anything but each other.

"What was that?" Tao asks after an age has passed, maybe a millennium lost in Adam's eyes, in the way his cheeks are flushed and his mouth is redder than apples.

Adam raises a hand and pushes a stray strand of hair away from Tao's forehead. It catches one of the tattoos there and sends it buzzing with an appreciative hum.

"I kissed you. And you kissed me back," Adam says. And there's that smile, and gods, how good it looks like this, now Tao knows what it tastes like.

Adam ducks forward and presses a tiny butterfly kiss to the corner of Tao's mouth, and Tao chases it, but it's gone almost too quickly.

"You kissed me," they say. "Nobody's ever done that before."

And it's true. They've never sought it out, never imagined they could kiss someone. Never imagined it could feel as safe as it just did. Never imagined how it could feel to be that close to another human being and share that with them.

Their power still thrums, oddly sated yet not, jittery under their skin like hour-old caffeine.

"I refuse to believe that," Adam says, and he seems just as dazed as Tao is. "How could nobody—they must all be mad. Or blind. Or both. No, that's no excuse. There are no excuses. Look at you."

"Honestly," Tao says, though they know Adam believes them. It's almost to themself that they say it, looking back on twenty-one years and the sheer lack of touch there has been since their power manifested when they were a teenager and they locked themself away, certain that touch was dangerous, something not to be played with.

And yet here they are.

"I should have asked," Adam says, and Tao shakes their head.

"No, I knew. I think I knew the second I saw you. That you were going to kiss me. That I *wanted* you to kiss me." A big confession. In a small room, surrounded by illegal books.

Adam seems to realize where they are at the same time Tao does, and grins a little more crookedly.

"And in front of Mary, no less. She'd have words for us. I can only imagine what she'd think of that."

"A bit of scandal. She was used to that, from what you've told me," Tao says, trying to match Adam's sun-powerful smile.

"True, true enough. Let me put her away, though. Do you want to—there's a park, not far from here. We could go there. It's nothing special, but it'll be empty. We could... talk?" Adam asks, a little uncertain now. He busies himself with packing the books away, not looking directly at Tao.

"I'd like that." Tao doesn't want this night to end, but in the back of their mind they remember the promise they made to themself, a promise they want to break, a promise that could stretch, couldn't it? A little longer, a few more days?

A lifetime?

"You look a million miles away," Adam says. He squeezes Tao's gloved hand in his, fingers linking loosely through Tao's.

"I'm right here," Tao says, and then they are. In an archive room with a beautiful boy who wants to kiss them. They're right there.

Adam walks them out of the library, hands still interlinked, and

Tao notices how their strides are almost equal, each step perfectly in time. *You could have this*, their brain whispers treacherously. *If you weren't so afraid, you could have this all the time.*

It's not true, though, could never be true, and their heart nearly breaks with it.

Adam lets go of their hand to pull open the heavy main door and then to use the tiny key to lock up behind them.

"It's not a real key," he says as Tao watches. "It doesn't do anything. Not physically. There's nothing it connects to. But most people use charm codes to lock the door. I just—there's something solid about having a real key."

The words are half-truths, even to Tao's ears. They could tell Adam that they know, that they've tried to find out why Adam doesn't seem to have access to magic in the same way the rest of the world does. They could tell him that it doesn't make them think any differently of him, or any less. They could tell him everything—the feeling of growing up with a power, or lack of, that could ruin your life.

But they don't, because this is only for tonight. They've already crossed so many lines, and they can't cross any more.

Instead they reach out and take Adam's hand. The warmth of his palm seeps through the wool of their glove like captured flame, causing their power to curl around it like an animal exhausted after a long hunt.

"You don't like being touched," Adam says, not moving, just looking down at their joined hands. "When I first met you, you actively shied away from me."

"I trust you," Tao says. "More than I can say for most people."

Adam's smile looks a little sad. He squeezes Tao's hand and asks, "Were you lonely?"

Tao thinks about their apartment, a bed big enough for two but filled only with one, going to sleep alone and waking up alone. Days spent by themself when they weren't working. The way they could walk through the city surrounded by strangers and not talk to another living soul.

"Yeah," they say.

"I was lonely too," Adam says. "I tried so hard not to be, but I was. But not now. Not right now."

Tao tightens their grip on Adam's hand, and Adam leans his shoulder against theirs. This ridiculous, temporary, liminal thing is going to eat Tao alive. They would die for this boy; they would kill for him.

They would cast him free, and that will hurt the most.

They both start walking, Tao taking a second to look over their shoulder back at the library, the grandiose façade of it, not imposing but welcoming. They wonder if they'll ever be able to return here or whether Adam will haunt this place as readily as any ghost.

What Adam had told them, what Adam had shown them about Mary Mallon, the born necromancer who did no harm, who raised only her daughter and even then, even filled with the worst kind of grief, was kind—Tao doesn't know what to make of it. That there exist in the world people who are sympathetic to necromancers, people like Adam, who know about this dreadful power, the utter taboo of it, and who aren't afraid but want to help. *To make things better.*

In another lifetime, Tao would tell him everything—about the way that, even as they walk, palm to palm, shoulders brushing, the contact points cause their power to scream with want. Like a moth to torchlight, their power bumps again and again and again, trying to understand the way Adam can exist and how readily his life force burns before them. How easily snuffed out.

They reach the park, Adam not trying to fill the silence, his own eyes not tracking, like he too is thinking hard. Tao remembers noticing the swing set and guides them both to it, and Adam smiles again then and sits down on one creaking sun-bleached swing as Tao takes the one beside him.

Above them, the night sky has revealed itself—a blanket of black dotted with stars, the moon low and heavy and yesterday-full. The same moon Pru harvested her charcoal under, but different now, less than it was, doomed to keep getting smaller until something shifts and it grows strong again.

Tao scuffles their feet beneath them, and with a creak of the metal links that hold the swing seat, they push off, a small sway back and forth. Each movement is accompanied by the strained sound of rust on rust, but the swing itself is steady, charmed not to break, so despite how it looks like it could fall apart, it won't.

It won't.

"I wish I could tell you about the stars," Adam says. "It feels like something I should be doing right now. But I don't know anything. I wish I did."

Tao doesn't either, but the sentiment moves them.

"Make something up," they say. "Make something up about the stars."

Adam pauses for a moment, head tilted upward, swinging gently with one foot on the ground, ankle twisting to cause momentum.

"Okay," he says. "This is what I know. The stars are very far away, impossibly far away. We'll never see them in our lifetime, never really know them. The sun is the closest star, but not the biggest by far. And it warms us during the day and offers us the moon at night—a brother perhaps, or a lover. We're never alone, even when we think we are."

Adam pauses, biting his lip, clearly thinking hard. Tao watches him in awe, blinking slow, wanting to capture this moment and every moment.

"Every star is potential. Every star could be another planet's sun. Every star out there could mean that a million billion miles away there are two people sitting on a swing set just like us, making up stories about the universe. And maybe they're afraid that they're too small to make a difference, or maybe they're afraid that there's nobody else out there. But they look up at their own night sky, and they're looking right at us. A million billion miles away and they're right there. And maybe they're in love. Or hoping to be. Maybe tonight their lives changed a little, became a little brighter. Maybe they're less alone now than they were when they got up this morning. Maybe they're looking upward, when really, they want to turn their head and look to the side, because the universe is full, teeming with life, but the only person they want to know is a foot away from them, and they're so scared and so hopeful, and the universe is rooting for them too."

Adam finishes and turns to look at Tao.

"You believe that?" Tao asks, and Adam stops swinging.

"It's a story," he says, a little carefully, sounding a little guarded.

"All stories are rooted in truth," Tao points out, because they are, aren't they?

"Then yes," Adam says after a few seconds. "I want to believe the universe is rooting for me. For us."

"Even though we're very small?"

"Especially. Because of that. The universe looks at all the small things she has created and wants the best for them. Why else would she make them?" Adam asks.

Tao reaches across for the metal of the links that hold Adam's swing and pulls him close enough that they can reach across and capture his mouth with their own. They don't believe the universe gives a damn about them, but for a brief moment, they can imagine that it does, and all because Adam told them it's so.

When they pull away this time, they hate themself a little more for prolonging this, for deepening it. For wanting so damn much. Adam looks at them, and they forget how to breathe, as though they've never done it before.

"I don't know how to believe in a benevolent universe," they say, "but I believe in you." And that hurts the most. Because they do. They believe in Adam in a way they can't put into words. They can imagine falling asleep in his arms and waking up and his face being the first thing they see. They can imagine shared shopping trips, shared lazy afternoons, and a thousand shared kisses. They can imagine it all, sprawling out easy and slow across the decades.

"I'm so glad I met you," Adam says, unknowingly twisting the knife.

"Walk me back to my apartment?" Tao asks, pushing again, against themself, against the boundaries they've set. *Just a little longer, just a little more.*

"Now?" Adam replies.

Tao looks at him, then back at the stars.

"In a little while," they say. "Tell me more about the universe."

And Adam spins stories out of stars and constellations and comets and moons. He pauses every so often to reach across and press a soft kiss to Tao's mouth, or cheek, or even their nose. And then he carries on, dozens of alien worlds just like theirs but slightly different, and on each one, a couple of people are looking up at the sky and feeling less alone.

Tao rests their head against the chain links and swings gently, and Adam covers their hand with his, holding them safe, like gravity, lest they drift off into space.

CHAPTER TWELVE

TAO IS still holding Adam's hand when they arrive outside their apartment building, and they fancy they can feel his pulse thrumming through them, connecting with their own and echoing back. They feel anxious, uncertain, and their brain runs a mile a minute as they wonder, *Will I invite this boy up to my apartment?*

They pause, and Adam stops walking and smiles.

"Look at you," he says and raises their joined hands to touch the tattoos at the very tip of Tao's hairline. "Can I ask—about—the other ones?"

"I don't want to talk about it. Is that okay?" Tao says. Adam, gods, Adam just smiles, a little sadly, and nods.

"Of course, gods, of course. They just—they look sore. I don't want you to be hurting."

"I'm not, not right now," Tao says with Adam's skin against theirs, the warmth a furnace against the cold night air.

Adam looks up at the apartment building, the red brick, slightly faded outside, hiding a dozen homes, a dozen lives.

He lights up when he spots something, and Tao turns to look. He's seen the crudely drawn foxglove Tao etched into the brickwork a couple of years back—protection.

"You did that," Adam says, and it's a statement, not a question.

"Yeah," Tao admits. "I suppose, well, it's what I do."

"That's amazing," Adam says, and Tao doesn't know how to reply. Adam continues, shaking his head as if in wonder, "Can I see you again? Tomorrow?"

"Not tomorrow," Tao says, "I have—something." *Spaghetti Saturday with Luis. Which sounds so silly but matters so much.*

"Mysterious, tell me more," Adam teases, and Tao can't resist, can't resist that smile, those eyes.

"Spaghetti Saturday. My neighbor, Luis, I help him cook sometimes. He's teaching me his grandmother's recipes. When I moved in, the very first day, he came over to complain because I closed my door too loudly. I think he saw how alone I was. He sort of adopted me, I suppose. And now he's the closest thing to a grandfather I've ever known," Tao says, words tumbling out, filled with warmth and love for Luis, the man who accepts them fully and welcomes them into his life, into his home.

"Spaghetti Saturday? That's the most adorable thing I've ever heard," Adam says. "I might actually die from how cute that is."

"Don't," Tao says, holding Adam's hand a little tighter. "Don't do that."

"Don't worry, it was just a joke. Besides, I could always get ol' Mary to bring me back, right?" Adam laughs a little, and Tao's stomach turns over.

They imagine Adam, not as he is now, but as the empty husk he would be, could be, if that happened. Glazed-over eyes and hanging limbs, a puppet waiting for strings to be pulled. It's the worst thing they've ever thought of, and they suddenly feel very sick.

"Hey, hey," Adam says, noticing how pale Tao has gone. "Just a bad joke. I know it doesn't work like that. Hey, come here."

Adam gathers Tao to him, wraps his arms around Tao's waist and rests his chin on Tao's shoulder. Tao breathes him in, breathes in the life of him, wanting to relish this, because his words have crystallized Tao's every thought about all tonight could be, all it could ever be.

They can't ignore that there's a necromancer on the loose in the city. They can't ignore that they themself are a necromancer. They can't ignore the dreams. They can't ignore the way it's going to end—in dirt and death and decay.

They let out a small sob, involuntary, and Adam holds them tighter.

"Really bad joke, huh?" he asks, and Tao nods against him. They don't want this to end, and it feels so cosmically unfair that it has to. And they know how much it will hurt Adam… what they have to say to make him leave.

But they have to protect him. He's so godsdamned important. He's every star in the sky, every constellation, shining so bright.

"I should go inside," Tao mumbles, and Adam pulls back a bit to hear them.

"Are you okay?" he asks, and Tao shakes their head, honest in this, at least. Adam frowns, and his face isn't designed to frown, Tao decides. It looks wrong on him, and they want to fix it, wipe it clean and make him smile again.

"You're not okay," Adam says. "Why aren't you okay?"

"I can't see you again," Tao says. "Not tomorrow, not ever. It's only tonight. It has to be only be tonight."

Adam chews on his bottom lip, arms still on Tao's waist but looser now. His brow furrows as he tries to understand.

"What do you mean? Tao, I don't understand."

"This, us, it can't be a thing. It can't. It's not safe. You're not safe," Tao tries. How much can they say without putting Adam in danger? Adam, who seeks out books about necromancy for fun? Adam who might try to solve this mystery too.

"I don't know what you mean. Tao, tell me what you mean. I'm safe. Why wouldn't I be safe? Look." He lets go of Tao's waist and pulls up his sleeve to show the wolfsbane tattoo. "You gave me this. So that I'd be safe. That's what you do. That's your job. So tell me, why aren't I safe?"

"I can't tell you," Tao says, their voice cracking as they speak. They need this to be over, but Adam won't leave. Why won't he just walk away? Why is this so hard?

"Please try," Adam says, and there's pleading in his voice now and that awful look on his face. He's sad, Tao thinks. He's so sad.

Tao points to the ugly raised tattoo Pru etched into their face and how it feels like a lifetime ago now.

"I got this because I thought it would protect you. That's the truth of it. And look—look what happened. My body rejected it, and I nearly died. Zeke saved me. That's what the others are for. All those tattoos, all those charms, because I'm so dangerous my power would rather kill me than be erased. If it'll do that to me, imagine what it'd do to you."

"You were trying to protect me," Adam says, latching on to that and ignoring the rest. "Tao, can't you see what that means?"

Tao shakes their head.

"It's not safe. You're not safe with me," they say, trying different variations of the same thing, begging for Adam to understand and just go.

"I don't believe you. I know what it's like not to feel safe. I know because I've felt it my entire life. Up 'til now. I feel safe with you, Tao, I do. And I don't think there's any part of you that would ever willingly harm me."

"Stop saying my name," Tao says, and Adam looks sadder still. "You don't know me."

Adam lets out a slow sigh.

"I don't know you. You're right. But I want to. I wanted to know you from the first moment I saw you in the coffee shop. I watched you, you know? I thought to myself, gods, if I could get the courage to go speak to them, if they ever noticed me—but you never did. Until yesterday. And when you did? It felt like I was seeing in Technicolor for the first time. And you talked to me. Tattooed me. Passed on that protection to me."

"It's my job. Like you said," Tao grits out.

"Is this your job? Do you go on dates with all your clients? Do you kiss all your clients? Do you have all your clients make up stories for you? Do you invite all your clients to walk you home? No, I don't buy that. This isn't what you want," Adam says, and confusion is writ wide over his face, but determination too.

"You don't get to decide what I want," Tao says.

"Well then neither do you!" Adam bursts out. "You don't get to decide if I'm safe with you or not. That's for me to decide. It's not a choice you get to make for me."

Tao is exhausted, sick to their stomach, and they feel ugly, so ugly in the presence of this boy who cares so deeply he's willing to fight for them.

"I don't know what to say," Tao says slowly. "I've made up my mind."

"I don't think you have," Adam replies. "I think you're scared. And I'm trying to understand why."

"Because this isn't easy!" Tao exclaims. "You're trying to make it easy and it's not. It can't be. It never will be. You'll always be in danger, and I can't keep you safe all the time. I'm doing this for you."

"You know, when people do things for me, they're normally

nicer about it." Adam sounds as tired as Tao feels. "I'm not expecting this to be easy. Relationships aren't easy. But I at least expected you to try. I thought we were worth trying for."

"I guess not," Tao says, and it hits their teeth and makes them want to hiss and take it back.

"You don't mean that," Adam replies.

"What do I have to say to get you to leave?" Tao asks, because Adam is planted like a tree, solid in every way Tao isn't.

"Tao," Adam says softly, calm now. He steps closer again, and once again runs his hand down Tao's face, careful not to nudge the fresh tattoos there. "I can leave if that's what you really, truly want, but it wouldn't be the end. Think about tonight. Think about us. What we could be. And consider letting us be that. I know it's hard. It's all hard. Gods, it's all so hard. But I trust you, Tao. I feel safe with you. I'll keep saying it until you believe me. Please believe me."

Tao takes a step back, then another. Adam drops his hand to his side.

"I can't. I'm sorry, but I can't. Adam—please." Their voice cracks again on Adam's name. "If you really trusted me, you'd trust me on this."

"But it's not real," Adam says, sounding defeated, finally. "It's not what you want."

"I'm trying to keep you safe. That's what I want," Tao says. *Not a cold, dead thing. Not an empty shell. Not congealed blood and torn muscles and graying skin.*

"I still don't understand," Adam says, but Tao can see the exact moment he gives in. He seems to become smaller, farther away.

"I know. I'm sorry," Tao says, meaning it fully.

"I'll come back, you know," Adam says. "I'm not giving up on this."

"Please," Tao begs.

"I had a really nice night." Adam's smile is sad, small, barely there. "You should know that. I had a really nice night."

He turns then and starts to walk away.

Me too, Tao thinks, *me too*.

They're about to turn and enter the building when Adam turns and calls out, "The foxglove carved into the brickwork. Who's that protecting? Just you?"

Confused, Tao answers. "The building. Everyone in the building."

"Isn't that your answer, then?" Adam starts to walk away again. Tao watches him leave, not sure what he meant. Of course they protected the entire building. They care about the people who live there. Why wouldn't they want to keep them safe?

They rub their gloved hand over their wet cheeks and go inside, sniffing and trying to hold back more tears. They walk slowly up the three flights of stairs, dragging their feet, feeling as much like a corpse as any dead raised soul.

They reach their apartment and half expect to see Luis waiting for them, not that they'd know what to say to him. Not that they deserve it.

Their wards welcome them and coo over them in concern.

Tomorrow they'll find the other necromancer and end this one way or another. They can't put it off any longer. People are dying. It was nice to pretend, but they can't anymore.

This is their city, their home. And it's kept them safe.

It's time to return the favor.

Outside the building, three bodies tilt their heads in a parody of curiosity. Their necromancer stands between them and stares up as the light at Tao's window goes out.

It's nearly time.

CHAPTER THIRTEEN

DIRT—DIRT CHOKES Tao's lungs and blurs their eyesight, caving in as they run and scramble and try to free themselves. Shards of white bone, hollowed out and empty now, scatter and trip them, ribs and femurs and thighs, and a skull, smiling and proud, stares up at Tao. A burst of blue flame, and it should be cold but it's artificially warm, not real fire, a shallow mimicry of it. A voice speaks words Tao can't make out, something about a boy, something about a boy who is important. A hand in theirs—they look down and it's a husk of a thing, withered skin and too-yellow fingernails. Eyes meet theirs and scream silently, and then the awful crack as the ground beneath them both dissolves, rips apart at the seams, and then the horrific march of boned feet on earth.

They recognize those eyes.

"I trust you."

"It'll hurt like hell."

Knocking—

Knocking.

Tao wakes up. Somebody's knocking on their front door—three knocks, then two. Luis's knock.

Tao swears, blearily grabs their phone, and looks at the time. It's just gone noon, so no wonder Luis has become impatient with them. They drag themself out of bed and to the door and pull it open to reveal Luis's smiling face.

"Terrible child!" he exclaims, then looks Tao up and down. "Oh dear, what a mess you are!"

Tao went to bed in last night's clothes, and now they think about it, forgot to take their braids out too. It's a fair assessment, then.

"You're always so nice to me, Luis," they say, and Luis chuckles.

"Last night was a good night, then?" he asks, and Tao immediately wants to cry, because *yes, no, not really.* Luis must read it on their face because his demeanor shifts and he becomes every inch the grandparent Tao has built him up to be as he steps past Tao's wards and into the apartment to hug them. And much as they'd normally resist, they're so damn tired.

They've never hugged Luis before, or anyone really, besides Adam and Pru, and they can't help but compare the two. Adam was firm, and his hugs were strong and felt powerful, despite everything. Pru hugs like she does everything, fleetingly, briefly, like a butterfly wing flapping before flying away. Luis's hug is frail. His small arms pat Tao on the back and remind them of a bending branch, like Luis could snap at any second.

Their power remains quiet, not leaping or watching like it does with Adam. *Did.* Did.

Not anymore.

"Today's not really a good day," Tao murmurs when Luis releases them, and Luis scoffs at the notion like it's utterly ridiculous.

"It's Spaghetti Saturday. What other day are we supposed to hold it on? And besides, the ingredients are ready and waiting for you. You wouldn't keep good food waiting, would you?"

Tao shuffles their feet, not wanting to look Luis in the eye. They had planned for today to be the day they finally faced up to everything they'd been avoiding—the necromancer, for one. They can't just spend a leisurely afternoon cooking like things are normal.

A last meal, before the cops blow your brains out.

They'd love to believe Adam's certainty about *no weapon forged by man* and all that, but the truth is necromancers die all the time at the hands of the police, and if Tao is seen to even consider using their powers, even if it means stopping the rogue necromancer, it's a death sentence.

So maybe they deserve Spaghetti Saturday. They look at Luis's face and feel fierce protectiveness and love.

"Just give me five minutes," they say, and Luis nods sharply.

"I'll give you ten," he says, generous to the last, and looks around Tao's apartment. "You do not have much, do you, terrible child," he observes.

It's true. Tao's apartment is hardly decorated, and definitely not to any aesthetic standard. It's a place to live more than a place to come home to. After moving around so much as a child, they're still a bit uncertain about setting down roots.

"Redecorating," they say instead, because it's less sad.

Luis nods, but it's clear he doesn't believe them.

"Ten minutes." He salutes Tao and then pulls the door closed.

Tao shuffles through to the bathroom, brushes their teeth, combs out their hair, and stares again into the mirror at the new tattoos, now almost a day old and already healing, less red than before, less angry—all aside from that terrible first one, which still stands red and sore and barely legible. Tao touches it gently with a fingertip and recoils at the sharp sting of pain that results.

They pull on old jeans and a hoodie, knowing they'll likely get splashed by food. They really need to do laundry. Most of their clothes have been worn now, and they add to it to the mental list. Then they remember.

They're going to hunt down a necromancer and probably die. Laundry can probably wait.

They don't grab any food because they know Luis will feed them well, and they head out the door and across the hall to the door to Luis's apartment, which swings open, the door unlocked for them.

Luis is already at the stove, stirring a pot that smells of onion and garlic, which makes Tao's mouth water.

"Vegetarian mince, and later, vegetarian meatballs, yes?" Luis says, not really a question at all. "We want to do as little harm while we're on this earth as we can."

"Yeah," Tao agrees, thinking back to last night and wondering if they made the right choices, said the right words. In another world, perhaps, they could have explained all the truth of it, told Adam every scary thing and had him listen, understand, and then leave because he understood entirely the threat at hand. But it's not that easy.

Being with Tao would always be dangerous to him. While this is the first other necromancer Tao has encountered, that doesn't mean there aren't others out there. Is Tao supposed to ignore them all when they're the only one who can sense it, can pick it up first?

They've been so negligent. They should have followed the trail that first day, no matter how muddied it was. They should have sent out that wisp of magic to drop the body wherever it stood, even if it did alert the other necromancer. They should have done more, and done it sooner.

It's not your job. Then who? The police, who will go in guns blazing and burn any dead that stand, and burn the necromancer too if they can? The police, who will suffer losses as the necromancer fights them? The police, who will raze the ground so that nothing can ever grow again?

Tao may be uncertain of their power, but they know they can do better than that, have to believe they can do better than that. At least they can put the bodies to rest. At least.

"Stir," Luis interrupts their thoughts and hands them a wooden spoon, "and don't let it burn."

Tao stirs as Luis adds ingredients and lowers the heat to allow it all to simmer and bubble. It smells incredible, especially to Tao, who is hungry now, having skipped both dinner last night and breakfast today.

"You told me you had a date, yes?" Luis says, and Tao fumbles with the spoon, the hypnotic action interrupted. "It went badly?"

Tao sighs.

"It went really well, actually. He was perfect. But—it's the wrong time. For us."

"Love is on a schedule now?" Luis muses, and Tao blushes a little. It wasn't love. It could have been, maybe, in a few months or so, but it wasn't yet. It had been a seedling, pushing out of the soil, and Tao had trampled it and crushed it back into the dirt.

"Not love, Luis," they say. "And no, not really, but it's complicated."

"You know how long I was married, terrible child?" Luis asks, and Tao knows, because Luis speaks often of his wife and their long life together. The framed photos are all over the apartment still, her knickknacks still scattered across the shelves. "Fifty-six years. Fifty-six years, terrible child, and all of them complicated in their own way."

"This is different," Tao tries.

"Of course it is," Luis says, like it's obvious. Perhaps for him it is. "It's always going to be different. But by the gods, does that mean you give up? Terrible child, I thought you knew better than that. And keep stirring."

"He thinks I'm something I'm not," Tao says uncertainly, because they're not so sure that's true. Adam seems to see them pretty clearly, actually. Adam probably would accept the awful truth of their power. He would probably even accept the way Tao's power wants him, might even be flattered. Gods, what a thought.

"And what does he think you are?" Luis prods as he takes the spoon from Tao's hand and hustles them out of the way when the pot begins to sizzle. "It's burning, terrible child!"

"I'm sorry, Luis," they say, moving to one side. "And—I don't know. He thinks I'm safe. Someone safe. And I don't think that's true."

Luis tuts, mutters under his breath for a minute, and then turns to face Tao.

"Terrible child. What are you doing right now?"

"What do you mean?" Tao asks.

"You are standing in the kitchen of an old man, and you are cooking spaghetti. And you are telling me that you are dangerous. Is this what you are saying?"

"That's different," Tao says again.

"So you say. And I say—pah. Excuses. That's what you're doing, you're making excuses. It is okay to be scared, terrible child. Perhaps even dreadfully so. But do not destroy a good thing out of fear that it could be good. This spaghetti will be so tasty you will eat too much of it and your stomach will ache. Does that mean we should stop making it? Just because something is good now but might hurt later, does that mean it is not worth the good? Fifty-six years. And then ten of missing her like I have lost a limb. But you know, terrible child, I would not trade away the good years just because now there are some bad ones. We must accept all that the universe gives us and be glad for the days the sun shines on us, even if the next day it rains."

Sunshine. Sunshine smiles and the impossible way Adam's face would light up. Glasses slipping down his nose and the way he always seems to be wrapped up in too many layers. The way he kisses with such certainty, guiding Tao through it. Two people, looking up at the stars, wondering if they were alone and hoping they weren't.

"Did I make a mistake, Luis?" Tao asks. They already know the answer. If they survived the encounter with the other necromancer, they could have found Adam after. Explained it all. Now they can't do that. Can they?

"You are so young," Luis says softly. "You are allowed to make mistakes. It is what you do next that reveals who you truly are."

"I was trying to keep him safe, but instead I hurt him anyway," Tao realizes. Maybe even hurt him more than they ever could have with their power, the power that seemed to be growing more accustomed to him with every touch, every kiss. Like exposure therapy, like being around Adam was the cure to the potentiality of harming him.

"That's so often the way," Luis says. "We think we know what is best for other people, but we cannot. Only they are allowed to decide. Surely, if my wife had listened to me, we would never have been married."

"Really?" Tao asks, surprised. Luis has never mentioned that before.

"I had just arrived on the continent, and perhaps I should say views were less enlightened then. To fall in love with a foreigner? Her parents were outraged. They forbade it. Asked her to choose. Of course she did no such thing, sneaking out to see me while playing good to them. And of course it ended in hurt, and I told her to go back to them. And she told me that she was making her choice. That I was her choice. And that if I took that away from her, then she would never forgive me."

"So her parents abandoned her? For choosing you?" Tao asks.

Luis's smile is crinkly and bright.

"That's the thing, isn't it? They never did. Because when you really love someone, you can't just stop. They accepted me in the end. Accepted that she loved me. They were never as happy about it as they would have been if she had married anybody else, but she didn't marry anybody else. She married me. The stomach ache wears off, you see? You think it won't, that it'll go on forever. And then, one minute to the next, it'll fade without you realizing. And you won't even notice. Even hurt can give way to good, Tao."

Luis never says Tao's name, always referring to them as "terrible child," a nickname borne out of love and frustration in equal measure.

"Luis—" Tao begins.

"You are not as terrible as I would have you believe. Maybe it is time you believed that too. Now it is time to eat and to make our stomachs ache."

Tao grabs the plates and wipes their eyes surreptitiously as they do so.

And then they eat, and Luis is right, their stomach aches like it might burst from all the good food. But as they watch an old movie on the couch and watch him laugh at jokes they don't understand, they realize, *oh, it doesn't hurt anymore.*

CHAPTER FOURTEEN

THE SUN is setting by the time Tao gets back to their apartment, feeling pleasantly full and oddly at peace with the world. They're not entirely sure what they're going to do, but worrying about it feels foolish, like it'll do no good.

Despite everything, it's been a good day, and if it's their last, that's okay too.

They sit down on the couch and pull off their gloves, flex their fingers and wonder about the power that dwells within them. Is it enough? Can it be? Years of lying dormant, waiting to be used—will it be an explosion, or will it fizzle out?

Tomorrow they'll wake up, head to the alleyway, and find the dead. From there they'll find the necromancer and end this. One way or another, this has to end.

They've been pretending for too long.

They let out a shaky breath they didn't realize they were holding and laugh a little at themself. It's such a ridiculous situation, and they should be so scared. But it's all been leading up to this, hasn't it? Haven't the dreams taught them this much? So why run? Why keep running when it's always going to be on their heels?

If they're to die, then they want to die doing good, lessening the evil in this world. And if they survive, well—they'll worry about that if it happens.

It won't, but for a brief moment, they allow themself to entertain the possibility.

They'll go to the library with the biggest bouquet of flowers they can find. No—too dramatic. Hot chocolate, and one of the muffins Adam likes so much. And they won't beg or plead, but they will ask for forgiveness. They'll tell—an entire life laid out in words.

It's nice to think about. They smile.

There's a knock at the door, and their wards perk up and curl around them, practically purring. Confused, because it's not Luis's knock, they get up slowly and cautiously to answer. It can't be any-thing bad. The charm they carved into the brickwork outside prevents evil intent from entering the building, and their wards would be going berserk besides.

They open the door, and Adam stands there—their Adam, but somehow looking a little smaller, a little sadder. He looks at Tao, and his face crumples. Then he lets Tao guide him inside, the bare skin of Tao's palm against his. It's the first time their hands have touched, and Tao can't help but wish it were under different circumstances. As it is, Adam looks ready to fall apart.

They don't sit. Instead, Adam stands a foot away from Tao and rubs at his face, and Tao waits for what he has to say.

"I was going to be angry with you," he says eventually. "I was so ready to be mad at you. I walked over here, full of this kind of righteous fury, and I was ready to scream and yell about how unfair you're being. And then I got here, and I saw you, and now I just want you to hold me."

It's impossible. It's all so impossible. And yet Tao takes him into their arms. and he fits like he was carved out of marble to do so. His arms wrap around Tao. and Tao's hands fit to his shoulder blades and rest against the smooth bones there.

Adam shudders against them, and Tao presses their nose to the side of his throat, feeling the loose curls at the nape of his neck brush-ing against their face. In what world could they have given this up? In what world could they have walked away from this?

Adam is home in a way nowhere or nobody has ever been, more than bricks and mortar, more than a place to rest their head. Adam is where they want to come back to. It has been three days, and Adam is their beacon in the darkness, drawing them back in.

"You're here," they say, in wonder, in awe.

"I couldn't be anywhere else," Adam replies, voice muffled, halting, croaky, like he's trying not to cry. "I didn't want to be any-where else."

They stand for a long while, the pair of them, just holding on to one another, the world outside darkening as time paces forward. But they're still, only moving to breathe. Statues caught in one perfect moment, two pieces of a whole, something rare. Something beautiful.

After a lifetime, maybe two, Adam pulls back a little, still not letting go. He looks at Tao, dark eyes finding Tao's, and just *looks*, like he's trying to find something. It seems like he does.

"I was going to be angry," he says again and shakes his head. "And I think I will be. Perhaps. But I realized how much I was asking. How I wanted it to be easy. To have one thing that could be. I've spent my whole life working twice, ten times as hard as everyone else to be considered equal. And I guess—I didn't want to have to work for this. I wanted it to just fall into place. Just this once. Because it felt like it should. And now I'm realizing how stupid that was, to ask someone you only just met to be that vulnerable. I haven't told you my secrets, so why would you tell me yours?"

"No," Tao says, "no, no, no. Please don't apologize. I know. That it could never be easy. But I made it more difficult. And I want to tell you why, I do. And after tomorrow, I can. I can tell you every-thing—beginning, middle, and end. I drove you away, and I shouldn't have. You trusted me, and I didn't listen. Didn't want to hear. There was this brilliant bright thing in front of me, and I couldn't see it. But I do now, I do see it. I see you."

"Do you mean that?" Adam asks, full of terrified hope.

"Yeah." Tao nudges their forehead against Adam's and feels the tingle as their tattoos react to Adam's skin. Their power stays dor-mant, waiting but not pacing, and it really was just a matter of allow-ing this, allowing themself to touch, to let someone in. They've shied away from it their entire life. No wonder it reacted the way it did. No wonder.

Their heart reacts in the same way. Their blood. Every nerve in their body. They're on fire. Adam sets them alight. He is kindling to a flame they thought they'd long since snuffed out.

"The way I feel around you terrified me. Terrifies me still. I don't know what to do with that. I don't know how to navigate that," they say. "I've spent my entire life without a map, and here you are. I found you, or you found me, or we found each other, and I don't know where I'm going. Where I want to go. Just that I want to go there with you. And I was so scared of hurting you. Because I know that I can. I have that inside me. And I want to tell you about it all. Soon. I will. I want you to know me. I want you to be able to trust me because you see it all, not just the bits I don't hide away."

Adam inches forward, impossibly closer, and their noses rub together, and Tao can feel Adam's breath on their lips, tickling, life in the air, and they breathe it in, breathe him in.

"I'm scared," Adam murmurs, his lips catching against Tao's as he speaks, a kiss that isn't a kiss. "I'm scared that I can't leave you. That I'd never want to. I kept thinking—how could you be dangerous? Round and round in my head. You told me you were cooking with your neighbor today, your grandfather, and I thought—is that something someone who is dangerous does? Spaghetti Saturday—gods, it all felt so absurd. And I got so mad at you. Because I don't think you see yourself. Not really. And I understand. Or I want to. I want to try. And I know—I know you were only trying to do what was best for me. And I hope I'll be able to understand that too. But you need to know." Adam presses the tiniest kiss to the side of Tao's mouth. "I need you to know that you won't get rid of me that easily. You saw me, in the coffee shop. And you kept seeing me. Nobody else has ever done that. Nobody else has wanted to. And maybe I haven't wanted anyone else to. Maybe I was waiting for you. So maybe I want this, and maybe you're right and maybe it's not safe. But I don't believe that. I'm here, and you're holding me, and I feel safe. And all I want you to do right now is kiss me."

Tao breathes in, breathes out, then nudges their mouth against Adam's, finding home, and kisses him, chastely, barely there, and pulls back a few inches before Adam chases it and turns it into something more, something that feels like it's pouring out of him and into Tao. And Tao gives it right back, opening their mouth and letting him in, inhaling sharply at the sensation, and gods—they hadn't realized how much they'd missed it, because if they had, they could have never stayed away. It's been twenty-four hours, and it feels like they're an addict who's been clean for years taking their first hit. It's intoxicating, it's everything, it's Adam—Adam burning into them and that fire cleansing them—and they feel clean, brand-new, and as his hands move to cup their face, their own hands find his hair, tangle in those brown curls, pull him closer, closer, ever closer, as though they could be one being, one soul.

Adam lets out small whimpers as he kisses, and he bites as much as he soothes. It goes on, and on, and on, and their bodies press together at so many points of contact that Tao can't count them, and it's gorgeous. It's the beginning and the end and everything in between.

If they die tomorrow, they'll die knowing this.

And they know, now, that they have to survive. Because they can't leave Adam behind again, can't lose this perfect thing, emerging half-formed but already taking shape, and gods, as Adam presses a thumb to their cheekbone, to the fresh tattoos there, the pain should hurt, but it doesn't. It's something else, something new, singing and bright and brilliant.

Adam pulls away reluctantly, then pulls back in, leaving kisses like a trail Tao needs to follow, and they do until Adam places a finger to their lips, and they kiss that too, and he laughs, and gods, they've missed that laugh, that smile.

"I didn't come here for this," he says with red-rose lips. "I wanted—I don't know. Not closure. But I wanted to understand. Promise me that I will?"

Tao takes his hand, squeezes hard, and then tangles their fingers together, bare palm against bare palm, somehow more intimate than kissing.

"I hope that you do," they say. Then—"I'm so glad you're here. I'm so glad."

"Me too," Adam says and leans into Tao again and holds them, sturdy and solid and safe.

They find their way to the couch. Tao sits, and Adam curls up with his head on their lap, and they run their fingers through his hair, wrapping curls around and letting them go. He sighs, finally content.

They could have lost this. It's still complicated. It could still all go up in flames. But they think back to what Luis said, about every day being complicated. And about the good after the bad.

After tomorrow, after they survive tomorrow, somehow, that impossible somehow, after the bad, they want to be everything for this boy. They want to fall in love with him. They're already halfway there. They can feel it with every beat of their heart.

"How did you know which apartment was mine?" they ask, curious suddenly.

"There's an oleander drawn in silver Sharpie on your door,"

Adam replies. "Who else could live here but you?"

"You recognized it?"

"I spent all night researching poisonous flowers after I got my tattoo. I got the feeling it might be useful. Guess I was right," Adam says.

"You were right about a lot of things," Tao says. *So many things.*

"And believe me, I'll remember that. I might even want it in writing. But right now, I'm okay with this," Adam says and smiles up at Tao.

It's a perfect moment, one Tao wants to keep forever.

But it's shattered by the piercing wail of their wards going off and a knock at their door—three taps, then two.

CHAPTER FIFTEEN

ADAM JOLTS upright from Tao's lap, his glasses askew, and scrambles to his feet, Tao close behind.

"What is that?" he asks, barely audible over the awful screeching.

"The wards, something's set off the wards," Tao says, tense, on edge, adrenaline pumping through them like ice water.

The knocking comes again, three, then two. Luis's knock.

"Gods," Tao says and takes a step forward toward the door. They don't want to. They don't want to open the door. There's nothing good there.

Adam makes to follow, but Tao holds a hand behind them, a motion for him to stay put. If they can just protect him—

They put their other hand on the doorknob just as the knocking comes again, and pull the door open.

It's Luis. It's just Luis. Smiling at them.

Except it's not, is it?

It's not Luis at all.

The thing that was Luis but isn't anymore is all blotchy skin and hazed-over eyes, and the smile is all wrong—not Luis's crinkled-up smile but something else, something that was pure and now has been turned wretched.

Luis is dead, and this thing stands in his place.

Tao staggers backward, bumps into Adam and grabs at him, grabs his arm and holds him behind them, keeping one arm out in front as though they can ward off the thing, Luis-not-Luis, by thought alone. Adam's saying something, but Tao can't make it out, can't hear themself think. And their vision is fuzzing at the edges because they thought they had more time, and they never thought—

Gods, *Luis*.

The thing that used to be Luis doesn't move, just keeps smiling that dreadful smile, and Adam is still talking. Tao focuses and tries to make out the words.

"What's going on? What's wrong with him? Tao, what's going on?"

Tao keeps a firm grip on Adam's arm, holding him in place, and closes their eyes, just for a second, trying to wish it all away.

"He's dead," they say eventually as they open their eyes again and stare straight at the body. Not Luis. The body.

The body, the dead thing, tilts its head like it's disappointed in Tao, something so familiar and so alien at the same time. Tao wants to scream and cry and break everything, to tear the world apart. *This isn't fair.*

"Gods," Adam chokes out. "What—how—Tao?"

"This is it, this is why," Tao says, keeping their eyes on the body, which is just—looking at the pair of them. Not moving, just watching. Not even watching really. Because it can't. It can't do anything. It's a puppet. It's a mimic. It isn't real.

But it looks real. It looks just like Tao's friend.

"Tao, what's going on?" Adam tries to step forward, and Tao tightens their grip and holds him in place, even as he tries to squirm away.

"This is what I was trying to protect you from," Tao says, voice rising as the wards continue to scream, as Tao's pulse continues to speed their heart too fast, like it's trying to force it right out of their chest. "This is it. Gods. Oh Gods. Luis."

"Luis?" They hear Adam say, sounding startled. "Oh no—oh, Tao."

Two hours ago they were watching that dumb old movie with him, listening to him quote the lines, trying to understand decades-old jokes. Now he is gone. Just gone. And standing there, wearing his skin, is this abomination, and Tao needs it to stop, just to all stop—the siren-wailing wards and the way the thing that could never be Luis again is looking at them, and the way Adam is pulling at them, trying to get their attention.

"Just stop!" They sob out a scream, and several things happen at once.

Something jumps—power, pure, untamed power, from Adam to Tao where Tao's hand is on Adam's arm, and it hits Tao like a lightning bolt and burns through them, like they're going to die unless they let it out and die if they do. It fills them up with unimaginable power, like nothing they've ever felt before. Adam gasps and sags, but the world is still turning, and Tao feels the power escape them, surging under their command.

The windows of the apartment blow in, scattering glass and letting in the night. The wards abruptly stop their screaming. The overhead light expands its glow impossibly wide, flickers violently, and just before it bursts... the thing that was Luis seems to dissolve, flaking apart and leaving behind a pile of—dust?

And then the light blows and darkness covers them, leaving Adam collapsed behind Tao, his arm still in Tao's grip.

"What the hell was that?" Adam manages between breaths. He fumbles for his phone, turns on the flashlight, and shines it to where the body had been standing, where only dust motes are left in its place. Tao collapses beside him, letting go of his arm now, feeling numb, looking at the tiny specks dancing in the glow of the torch light.

"Tao," Adam says, leaning his head against Tao's shoulder heavily, sounding exhausted. "Tao, I felt that. Gods, what did we do?"

"I don't know," Tao replies, not blinking, not moving, just staring, feeling utterly hollow. They don't have words for what just happened, they just know that it did, even if they can't explain it. They crawl forward, grab their own phone, and turn on their own flashlight to highlight the small pile that is all that is left of Luis.

They reach out for it, fingers shaking, and it's—ash. It's ash. A pile of ash.

"I felt power," Adam says behind them, and in the sudden quiet, his voice is trembling. "I've never felt that before. I gave it to you. Tao. Tao, please."

Tao can't think, doesn't know what to do. The other necromancer got past their protective charm and got into the building. They killed Luis. They sent him to Tao. And then they just—left him there. Almost like a gift.

"He's dead," Tao says, really realizing it. Their stomach turns over. They let out a harsh sob. "He's dead."

Adam moves behind them, places a hand between their shoulder blades, and Tao shrugs it off.

"Don't touch me," they say, defeated. This is what they were built to do. What their power was always built to do. To destroy. This is the dream made flesh. It's started.

"I—I really need to right now," Adam says, and Tao feels that touch again and remembers the surge of power that had leapt from him when they'd needed it most. Had they taken it? Or—no. That's not what happened, is it? They lean into Adam's touch, sit back on their heels, phone on the floor, casting shadows on the ceiling.

Adam is shaking. Tao can feel it, and they don't know how to help. They can feel the salt of their own tears on their cheeks, rolling down to the corners of their mouth. They don't know how long they've been crying or when they started, just that it seems like they might never ever stop.

"Somebody killed him," they say, and then, "I—I did this. I made him go away."

Adam lets out a shuddering breath and then replies.

"It wasn't him, not anymore. You know that. Tao, which are you?"

Tao turns to look at him in the darkness, not understanding the question.

"Blood or born, which are you?" Adam asks, voice breaking.

Oh, right.

Of course he'd figure it out. Of course. It's not difficult. And with everything he knows, it's not even a logical leap. It's just connecting the dots.

"Born," Tao says softly. Admitting it to someone for the first time in their life. Saying it out loud should feel like catharsis. It doesn't.

"And the other—the person who did this—they're, they're not. Right? They're blood?" Adam asks, staring at Tao as though he can see their soul. Tao wonders *what* he sees.

"Blood, somehow. I don't know. *I don't know*. I don't know how they know about me. I don't know how they got in. I don't know anything. I just—this is. This is what I was trying to tell you. That I'm dangerous. You could've been killed. What if they—what if they come after you too?" Tao can't form sentences anymore. Every word comes out like it's tripping over their teeth and into the night air.

"Okay, it's okay. It's all going to be okay." Adam rubs circles on

Tao's shoulder, trails fingers down Tao's arm, to their palm, skin on skin, connection—touch.

That feeling of being hit by lightning.

"What are you?" Tao asks, staring back at Adam now. "What did you do to me?"

Adam looks down, looks at where he's tracing the lines of Tao's palm with his finger.

"I don't know. Gods, Tao, I don't know. I don't know what that was. I didn't know I could do that."

"We need to—tell someone. I don't know. We can't—I can't. I thought I could do this on my own, but I can't. What do I do?" Tao begs, and Adam gathers them to his chest, lets them sob, lets it wrack through their body, violent and ugly.

"You're not on your own," he says, holding tight, like he might never let go. "I'm here. You're okay. It's okay."

Tao moves so that they can look at him, look at that face they've already fallen for, and they can see the silver lines of fallen tears streaking his cheeks too.

"I kept you safe," Tao says. "Didn't I?"

"You did," Adam replies immediately. "You did so good."

"I feel—I don't know. Like I can't feel anything. I know I need to—I need to call Zeke. Gods. I can't think." Tao grasps for their phone.

Adam steadies them, keeps a hand on their arm as they move, as they swipe to dial Zeke's number. Tao closes their eyes when Zeke answers, and Adam moves in closer, rests his forehead against theirs.

In halting, stumbling sentences, Tao tells him everything. Tells him about the thing that was Luis until it wasn't anymore, about Adam, about themself. Tells him they don't know what to do now. Adam holds them as they feel themself start to shake again, like their very bones are vibrating. Adam holds them through it all as Zeke tells them to wait for him to come to them. To try to be calm. To stay in the apartment. Adam holds them as Zeke hangs up and the line rings out, dead air all that's left.

"He's coming," Tao says. Though they know Adam overheard it all, it's comforting to say it aloud.

"He's the one from the studio, right?" Adam asks, and Tao nods, brushing their foreheads against one another's.

"He's the only one left. Who I can trust. Who might know what to do," Tao says, hoping it's true.

"You can trust me," Adam promises.

Tao offers up a watery smile.

"I know. I've known since the beginning. I'm sorry I was scared."

"Don't." Adam traces his fingers across Tao's tattoos, letting them spark beneath his touch. "I understand now. You had every right to be scared. Gods, I told you about Mary Mallon, and you must have been so afraid. That I'd guess. That I'd tell. You're so brave. To have stayed. I get it now, Tao. I get it."

"I've never hurt anyone," Tao says, and Adam shushes them.

"I know, I know, you never could," he says, sounding so sure, so damn sure.

"I think I'm going to have to, though. The other necromancer. They—Luis isn't the first person they've killed. There are—I don't know. Others. I don't know how many. I didn't know what to do."

"It's going to be okay," Adam says again.

"How can you say that?" Tao asks, breathing him in, breathing in those words.

"Because it has to be." Adam kisses Tao, small, barely there but something sacred, like a vow. "Because it has to be."

They sit in the ringing silence, wrapped around each other, and wait.

CHAPTER SIXTEEN

"DID HE have any family?" Adam asks after an interminable silence. The wind blows in through the broken windows, punctuating it with feral howls and frigid bursts.

"Luis?" Tao says, then shakes their head. "No, only me. His wife died ten years ago. He was old, you know? The kind of old where you're on your own because you've outlived everyone else. And he was teaching me his grandmother's recipes. I—gods, I never paid attention properly because I thought I'd have more time."

"That's how humans work," Adam says. "We all think we've got more time than we do. We have to or we'd be too scared to ever love anybody."

"And now there's nobody left to remember him," Tao says bleakly. "Nobody to miss him."

"There's you," Adam points out, and Tao hopes that it's true. Hopes that there's some way past this. Hopes there's a tomorrow. Something beyond the end of the world.

"Am I enough?" they ask, and it's not about that, not *just* about that. It's about everything—everything to come, everything they might have to do.

"Always," Adam replies, sounding so sure. Like he just knows. Like it's obvious. Like he knows completely what Tao is saying and is responding in time, conversations hidden under conversations.

Tao's wards pick up again, curious this time, as though wary after—after. But they don't scream. Instead, they merely watch, and Tao lifts their head to see Zeke silhouetted in the still-open doorframe.

"Kid," he says, and Tao tries to untangle themself from the mess of limbs that is Adam and themself and stands awkwardly. Adam stands too, a hand on Tao's elbow, constant contact.

"Zeke," Tao says, and it comes out broken.

"Kid," Zeke repeats and steps carefully round the small pile of ash to envelop Tao in a hug. It's warm and bearlike and exactly how

Tao would have imagined it if you'd have asked them to. "Kid, what have you gotten yourself into?"

Before Tao can answer, Zeke pulls away and looks over at Adam. "And you, well, I can't say I'm surprised to see you here. Second I saw you, I knew you'd be trouble. Calling me 'sir,' just knew it."

"Adam helped," Tao says, trying to explain, not wanting Zeke to—what? Send Adam away? "Something, somehow. I needed everything to stop. I was holding his arm. And his power hit me. It was— big. That sounds stupid, but it's the only way I can describe it. It felt big."

"And it amplified your own powers, yes?" Zeke asks, and Tao nods. "I'm not surprised by that either."

"I don't have any powers," Adam says quietly, a confession. "I never have. That was the first time I'd ever felt anything like that."

"Don't worry, kid, I'll explain everything. Every time I meet someone like you, you all think you're so special, or so broken, or both, and I have to tell you, that's not it. Now, you're giving me a migraine just looking at you. Stay where I can see you."

Adam shoots a look at Tao. He hasn't moved an inch since Zeke started talking. Tao shrugs.

"I don't—" Adam starts.

"You don't understand. I know, kid, I know. Your secondary power—the one that protects you, keeps you safe. You never wondered why nobody seems to notice you?" Zeke asks.

The incredible disappearing boy, Tao remembers, and something slots into place.

"I didn't notice you at the coffee shop, even though you'd said you'd seen me in there before. And I would have noticed you." Tao pauses, feeling themself blush. "I would have noticed you. But I didn't, not until you wanted me to."

"Exactly," says Zeke, clapping his hands together. "A defense mechanism. Protection. Rare, but not unheard of. Your primary power, in the wrong hands, it could be monstrous. It makes you a target. So you protect yourself. Your body protects you. Keeps you out of sight and out of mind. Flitting in and out of existence. Now calm down and let me see you."

Something shifts in Adam, and it's like he's become more solid, even down to his hold on Tao's elbow.

"That's more like it," Zeke says. "Can finally get a focus on you."

"What's my primary—I don't understand. Primary powers, secondary powers. What's my power?" Adam asks, voice a jumble of nerves. Tao's heart aches for him as they remember the searches they attempted that night, the closed-down forums and dead ends. The seized web pages. No wonder Adam was drawn to the library. It was his only hope to find out about himself. And even then—

"You're a conduit," Zeke says, the unfamiliar word holding meaning beyond what Tao can comprehend. "You take power in from all around you, and you store it. And then, like a tap turning on, when somebody needs it, it flows out of you, amplifying what they can do to an incredible degree. You have no empathy for other people's powers, this is true. But nevertheless, what you have is power in its rawest form. And it's a dangerous power to have."

"Because if I gave it to the wrong person, they could do something terrible," Adam says, voice steadier now.

"Terrible, but great in its magnitude," Zeke agrees. "So your secondary power hides you away, a secret in a box. Unnoticeable. I imagine you could stand right in front of someone and not have them know you were there. You're not invisible, it's not that. You're just, in the politest way I can put this, insignificant. Not worth paying attention to. And that keeps you safe."

"Tao kept me safe," Adam argues, and Tao knows, knows that it's a lot of information to take in.

"It's okay," they say.

"No," Adam says, "you did. You kept me behind you when that thing came in here. And before, that night—you've been trying to keep me safe the entire time."

"I imagine Tao has been able to sense your power on you," Zeke says, and Tao looks away from Adam quickly and back at Zeke, "Tao's power is the perfect complement to your own. Tao draws from the world around them just as readily as you do. Together, you create a harmony, feeding back into one another. Back and forth, building that power through sheer repetition. Like feedback on a microphone too close to a speaker, picking itself up."

Feedback loops, again.

"I could sense—something. It drove my power wild. Made me—want. I was so scared I would hurt him," Tao says, remembering those first touches, how wild their power had felt, how unstable.

"But it got easier, yes?" Zeke says. "You can touch him now."

Tao nods.

"You felt that?" Adam asks, and Tao nods again. "Gods, no wonder you were worried. What was it like?"

Tao thinks back, remembering.

"It wanted to eat you whole, take everything from you. But it did get easier. Every time you touched me, it got easier. Until I could touch you." *Until I could kiss you* hangs in the air between the two of them.

"Both of you sensing threats and responding accordingly. I'm not surprised," Zeke says calmly. "You subconsciously started to bounce off of each other before even realizing it. It would have felt unusual, to say the least."

Something occurs to Tao, something that didn't occur to them while they were on the phone, or until this very moment.

"You're not surprised. About what I am. Or what Adam is. Did you know?"

Zeke looks away, lets out a sigh, and Tao steels themself.

"I know a lot more than I'd like, kid. Always have. And yet always sought out more. This—isn't the surprise it should be." He sighs. "Do you have any candles?" he asks and gestures around the room. "I don't want to have this conversation by the light of our phones anymore."

Tao nods. Moves to get them. Adam stills them.

"You stay here, I'll get them. Where are they?" he asks.

"The cupboard beside the fridge. The matches are in the drawer above it."

"Okay."

Adam moves away, but not before squeezing Tao's elbow reassuringly.

"He's a good kid," Zeke says when Adam's just out of earshot. "Dragged into a whole lot of bad."

"I know," Tao says. "I don't know—I don't know what to do.

How to keep him safe. If they can come for Luis, they can come for him. He needs protection, more than I can provide. I might not even be alive tomorrow."

"I think you're doing just fine. And I think you're going to need him. If you plan to fight this necromancer, you're going to need to be at your strongest. You need his power, if he is willing to give it," Zeke says. "You've protected him so far. It's what you do."

"It doesn't feel like enough," Tao says.

"It never will," Zeke replies. "You love him. You'd die for him. You'll kill for him. And it still won't feel like enough. Because that's what it all comes down to. Being vulnerable. Letting people in. I told you not to repeat my mistakes. Let him in. There's a way through this. Don't let it be over until it's over."

"I don't know if I can kill someone." Tao watches as Adam wanders around the bare apartment lighting candles, the orange glows flickering and casting strange shadows as he moves. "I don't know if I'm supposed to."

"One life to save—hundreds? Thousands? It shouldn't be a difficult decision," Zeke says, like it's easy.

"Very utilitarian," Adam says, rejoining the conversation. "The greatest good to the greatest number of people. You're willing to sacrifice one life, no—you're asking Tao to *take* one life, to keep this city safe. Do you have any idea what you're asking of them?" The last words come out angry, biting. Tao reaches for Adam's hand, finds it, and Adam sends the smallest flicker of power through—comfort.

"I'm not asking Tao to do anything. It's a choice only they can make. We can leave it to the police, certainly. But this necromancer is targeting Tao. If the police fail, if the police fall, and I have no reason to believe they won't, because I can feel it, the power rising in this city, dreadful and awe-inspiring all at once. Tao, yourself, together, you stand a chance. You can beat this. I wish I could offer some alternative, but I can't. And I'm not going to lie to you and say that it's going to be something you can be proud of. That it'll be something that won't haunt you. But you have already seen your friend die. Others have died too, people you don't know, and that feels more abstract, yes. But there are people out there who have lost loved ones, just like you. If you wish to honor your friend, you'll fight to protect all of those who stand in harm's way. No matter the cost," Zeke says, sentencing Tao. Sentencing Adam.

"That's—manipulative. It's not Tao's job to fix this! Tao didn't start this!" Adam bites out, angry on Tao's behalf.

"It *is* my job," Tao says sadly. "Protection. Carved into everything I do. This city is my home, Adam. I have to keep it safe."

"I don't want to lose you." Adam presses his shoulder against Tao's. "I'll stand beside you, I'll fight with you, I'll lend you all the power I have, but I can't watch you die. I can't do that."

"I can't die, remember? Remember what you said? Mary Mallon. Right? No weapon forged by human hands can kill a born necromancer. How can they kill me? How can they possibly even try?" Tao says, not believing it themself.

"They can hurt you," Adam replies. "They can make you wish you were dead. They might know something we don't. They might know a way to kill you. You were talking like they would. Don't lie to me now, Tao. I know it's a possibility."

"Okay, it's a possibility. I've known that since the beginning. But it's okay. It really is. I was so scared. But I have to do this. *I have to*." Tao forces the last three words out.

"Promise me," Adam says, "promise me you won't do anything stupid. Promise me you'll protect yourself the same way you've protected me, protected everyone you've tattooed."

"I can't," Tao says honestly. "Because I don't know what I'm doing. And I don't know how to win this. Zeke? Tell me, can I win this?"

"I believe that you can," Zeke says solemnly. "Between you, you hold immense power. Dead bodies fall. They don't disintegrate. They don't turn to ash. You've already proven how strong you are. It's a bigger chessboard, but you still, with the right moves at the right time, can win. If I didn't believe in you, I wouldn't be here. I'd be somewhere else, talking to someone else. This isn't the first war I've fought. This is not even my first necromancer. I'm old, Tao, and I've lived through worse than this. You can too."

"Will you be there?" Tao asks, because they—they feel like a child, suddenly, wanting Zeke there just as much as they need Adam there.

"No," Zeke says, and Adam moves to argue, but Tao quietens him, echoing his power back at him, comfort gifted back. "If you fail, which is unlikely, and if the police are overrun, you need a second wave. That's me. I'm powerful too, Tao. Not in the same ways as you, and I hope to the gods I won't have to use it, but against a worn-down necromancer who has already fought two battles? I'm the last line of defense. You don't need me there. Trust me. You have what you need already."

"What about Pru?" Tao asks, jolting suddenly. "We need to call Pru. If they're targeting me, they could be targeting her. We have to keep her safe."

"Prudence is safe," Zeke says, and the words hang in the air oddly. "She'll be here soon."

"Why here? To help you?" Tao asks, because everything feels wrong suddenly, like Zeke knows something, like the world might just be about to fall apart.

"Oh," Adam says, and he must have figured it out. Tao knows, deep in their heart, but doesn't want to say it. Can't say it, because that makes it real.

"It's Pru, isn't it?" they say, feeling sick to their stomach.

Zeke nods.

CHAPTER SEVENTEEN

"PRUDENCE HAS always sought power." Zeke walks over to the broken window and looks down at the street below. "I have known this about her since she first walked into the studio. Always disappointed with what she was born with, the dreams of prophecy that offer nothing but vague insights. She wanted more, and I could only hope to persuade her to calm that desire, to focus her gifts on protection, on helping others. There are many ways to leave your mark on this world, I have told her, good and bad. To protect people, to save lives, that is a good path. But she went out of her way to seek out new powers, to extend her empathy to the limit, with every client that came in, every person she passed on the street. I have been watching her for a long time—five years—hoping that she would realize that it was no good, that it would end poorly. And then, three years ago, you walked in, and your power radiated off you, and of course, Prudence wanted."

"That doesn't make sense," Tao says, as though any of it does. "She can't have known what I was. Only other necromancers can sense one another's power."

"She tattooed you, kid," Zeke says, and Adam lets out a small noise.

"She spilled your blood, Tao. Gods, how long has she been tattooing you for?" he asks, and Tao thinks of every time Pru has left marks on their skin, how Tao trusted her to protect them and felt only comfort at the buzz of a machine in her hand.

"Since the beginning, almost. Three years," Tao says.

"She's been a blood necromancer for three years. Gods, no wonder she's powerful. She must be driven half mad with it," Adam says.

"You know a lot about this," Zeke says.

"I read," Adam replies simply, curtly. "You knew about her, though. And Tao. And you did nothing. Until now. And even now you're only talking. Telling us what to do. Why didn't you stop her?"

Nobody talks to Zeke like this; nobody dares to.

"You've tattooed Tao too, right? Are you a blood necromancer too?" Adam continues.

"No," Tao says, realizing. "The block. The block protected you. It's been protecting you. But that should mean you can't see our powers. It's a wall, right? It keeps everything out. Stops your empathy. Which means you should be blind to it. But you're not."

"Walls can have windows, kid. Doors too. As for why I did nothing—I had to have hope. I have told you I have dealt with necromancers before. I have seen them driven mad by it. And I have seen Prudence driven mad in the very same way. Is it foolish to say I wanted to save her? To protect her from herself?" Zeke asks, and Adam scoffs.

"You've been putting people, this whole city, in danger for three years. Three whole years. You knew about Tao, you knew the danger you were putting them in. And I can forgive you for keeping their secret. It's not yours to tell. But to allow them to unknowingly pass on blood magic? To infect someone else? To watch and to do nothing as it all unfolds, like some ambivalent god? Who gave you the right? Now you're asking Tao to kill their friend. Someone they've known and trusted for three years. Someone they've worked beside. You knew this would happen, and you did nothing. Explain it to me, because I don't understand." Adam is shouting, rage dancing off him in elegant strikes that ripple through Tao's skin.

"Adam, that's enough," Tao says, trying to calm him. Adam turns to them.

"Aren't you angry? He's manipulated you from day one. He's put you in danger. He's let you believe you were dangerous when really he's the one who's let it all fall apart around you. The blood has always been on his hands, not yours. Never yours. And you've been blaming yourself. You should be angry."

"She's my friend," Tao says simply. It's the only thing they can think about. The only thing they know.

"And he wants you to kill her! Tao, please. Can't you see this for what it is? An old man playing the part of a god and then asking someone else to fix his mistakes." Adam holds Tao's elbow tight, too tight, painfully. Tao's power hisses at the touch but then quiets.

"Would you prefer the cops do it? You told me, didn't you?

That it's a kind of fascism, the way they treat necromancers. A bullet to the brain. Put down like an animal. I know. I know it all. I know what they'll do to her. It won't be pretty. It might not even be quick. We're not human to them, Adam. And I'm beginning to wonder if we are to you," Tao says, and Adam wilts at the last sentence, and his grip loosens. Then he grasps Tao's hand.

"You're not the same as her," he says.

"So that makes it okay? I did this to her. I may not have known I was doing it, but I still did it. This is my fault," Tao says.

"For what? For not knowing? Did you know you could transfer your power through blood? Tao. Please. I'm sorry. I'm so, so sorry. But this is not your fault," Adam says, his power fluctuating against Tao's skin, bursts that Tao can't read, like emotions skittering between them.

Zeke is still looking out of the window, staring down at the street below.

"It's my fault," Zeke says. "Adam is right. There is nobody to blame here but me. I saw that power-hungry young girl and I thought I could help her. I was young once. I know how it feels. To want more. To not be enough. Perhaps I saw too much of myself in her. I let things slide. Turned a blind eye when I shouldn't have. And I'm sorry."

"You're sorry? That's it? There are casualties to your actions. Luis died because of you. Because of her. Because you didn't stop her. And how many others? How many are you willing to sacrifice while you wallow in your guilt? Will you be sorry when Tao has to kill her? Will that sorrow help? When I stand beside them and help them to win this, will I feel the benefit of that sorrow? Tao might not be angry, but I am. Inaction is complicity. You're complicit in all of this. I hope you know that. I hope it keeps you up at night. I hope it aches inside of you for the rest of your life, knowing that this is... All. Your. Fault." Adam angrily punctuates the last three words, and Tao can't help but watch him, beautiful in his rage, this boy whose empathy may be exactly the type of empathy Zeke had spoken of—gods, it feels like a lifetime ago now. The type of empathy that leaves you vulnerable. Defenseless. The type of empathy that allows you to love.

That's what's pulsing from Adam's palm to Tao's. Mixed in with bitter anger, there's love, fierce and protective and raw and new.

And Tao can only echo it back, all of it, trying to soothe the anger and amplify the love. They hope Adam can feel it.

"We're running out of time," Zeke says. "You can be as angry at me as you'd like tomorrow, kid, but tonight? Tonight is when it ends. All of this. My folly. My mistake. It has to end tonight."

He continues to stare out the window and doesn't turn to look at them.

"Why tonight?" Tao asks, because there will be time later for anger, hopefully. They need a plan, something they can achieve, something to do. Some way of fixing this.

"She sent you a gift. Your friend. Luis. Your building is protected from ill intent. Have you considered how she could have gotten in if she was planning to murder someone close to you? Have you considered her intent?" Zeke asks, still not looking at them.

It all comes down to intent. In every charm, the magic only holds because of intent.

"She—she didn't have ill intent when she entered the building," Tao says slowly, horrified as the words form in their mind and spill out into the apartment. "*A gift*. She didn't make it attack us. It just stood there. She could have tried to kill us. She could have killed the entire building and brought them up to us. But she didn't. Just Luis." Luis, who was old enough to have lost everyone, old enough to reach out to a scared eighteen-year-old and treat them like his own grandchild, to pass down recipes and trade jokes in the hallway. Old enough that no matter how much time Tao pretended they still had together, it was shortening by every second.

"She doesn't think—" Adam claps a hand over his mouth. "She doesn't think that was—some kind of favor? Something good? She can't."

"You know necromancers," Zeke says. "You seem to understand blood magic. Imagine three years of it, building up inside of you, warping you. Imagine how that changes a person. Imagine what that could make a person believe."

"But it was empty. They're all empty. They're just dead. She can't believe there's anything more to it than that. It must be power. It must be about power," Tao argues.

"Maybe at first it was about power," Zeke replies. "Maybe for a long time. But now? Now I think it's about something more. At some point it twisted inside her and led her to this point. Didn't you wonder why she tried to take your power from you?"

Tao raises a hand to that branded welt of a tattoo on the edge of their cheekbone.

"I asked her to," they say. "To protect Adam. She messed up. She cried. It was a mistake."

"Do you still believe in mistakes?" Zeke shakes his head, eyes still on the street. "If she removed your power, then she would take out the one player in the game who could reasonably stop her. I do not believe she meant to harm you. I believe she really thought she could amputate it. So yes, she cried. And yes, it was a mistake, to a degree. She didn't expect your body to react in the way that it did. I don't think she was trying to kill you. So it did upset her, yes. Because she is your friend. That's the worst of it. She still sees you as a friend. Which is why she gave you Luis. What does one necromancer get another necromancer as a gift? For her? The person they're closest to. Because how can something that is dead ever die?"

Tao's head spins, and they feel sick to their very bones. Their stomach aches, and they're reminded of Luis's spaghetti and how long ago that feels now—a lifetime ago, literally. Adam holds on to them and helps them lower themself to the floor. They want to curl up; they want to close their eyes and make it all go away.

"This is your choice," Adam whispers, close enough that Zeke can't hear. His breath tickles against Tao's ear. "It's all your choice. You don't have to do anything he says. You can leave. He said he's powerful. He's done this before. Let him handle this. It's his mistake. Let him be the one to deal with it."

Tao shakes their head.

"No." They turn their head and lean into Adam. Adam nudges his forehead against Tao's, and Tao feels safe for one second. "No," Tao repeats. "I need to do this. She called me—*little sibling*. It's my power doing this to her. Maybe I can… help her. Talk her down. Make her understand. Maybe there's more than one way to end this."

"You don't have to," Adam says, voice still low.

"I know," Tao replies and brushes the lightest kiss to Adam's lips. "I'm choosing this."

"Then I'm right beside you. To the end. Whatever happens. I'm choosing this too," Adam says as he closes his eyes. Tao closes their eyes too and breathes in sync with him, letting themself just exist for a little while longer.

"You should look out of the window," Zeke interrupts.

Tao opens their eyes, and Adam looks at them—brown eyes almost black in the candlelight. Tao nods, and Adam stands and pulls them upright with him. They move over to stand beside Zeke at the window and look down at the street below, just like he'd been doing.

Dozens of dead look back at them—old dead, new dead. Some are little more than bones, others almost indistinguishable from what they were when they were alive. They crowd the sidewalk and stare upward. Waiting.

Tao's phone buzzes—once, twice, three times. Texts from Pru.

Little sibling.

Are you coming out to play?

We're all waiting for you.

CHAPTER EIGHTEEN

"SHE'S WAITING," Tao says. They pass their phone to Adam, who lets out a small noise in the back of his throat—animal fear.

"She's really doing this, then," he says as he passes it back. Tao slips it into their pocket, feeling silly for doing so. Who else is going to message them now?

"Yeah," Tao says. "Looks like it."

"Zeke, if this falls apart, if I can't do it—you'll—you'll be kind, won't you? To her? In the end?" Tao asks—begs.

"I will," Zeke promises. His tired face shows every year of his age—older than Tao could imagine being.

It's not much, that promise, but it's something.

"We'll find you after?" Tao asks, because it feels like something they should say. Making plans. Plans they can't imagine in their head. The dream is dirt and death and decay. There's no happily ever after.

"You will," Zeke replies. "Now go to her. I believe she has provided you with an entourage to get there safely."

Tao's heart beats rabbit-fast. They look at Adam and wish they could gather him to them, but know they'd never let go if they did. Adam tilts his head in response. *Are you sure?*

Tao nods. *I'm sure.*

Tao looks down at the street below and all the dead there waiting.

They're ready.

"Okay," they say. "Okay."

They stand up straight, center themself, and try not to think about the thousands of ways this could end. They look at Adam, at brown eyes and brown curls and those glasses that almost frame his face, like a portrait. Almost too good to be true.

Adam follows Tao to the open door, and they reach back through the candlelit darkness to take his hand, looking for that light. They find it. Adam holds on tight, and with a final look back at Zeke, Tao leaves the apartment and heads for the stairs.

Luis isn't waiting to scold them on the landing. They were still half expecting him there.

They don't take the stairs two at a time, not now. Instead, every step feels impossibly steep, like they could misstep and fall, like they're hanging over the edge of a precipice. The three flights down to street level, to where the dead are waiting, seem to take an age.

Night is giving way to the first shards of morning light, and the dead are illuminated by it, skin and bones pale and unearthly. Adam shudders beside Tao, and Tao squeezes his hand and takes a sharp intake of breath at the smell. Rot and earth and something that could be magic hang stinging in the air around them. It's the smell from the alleyway, but a thousandfold.

It's the smell of that forbidden magic writ large, and the dead stare with blank, unseeing eyes at Tao and Adam as they step closer.

The crowd of dead parts, making way for them, and Tao glances at Adam as they walk into their midst. They have to believe that Pru doesn't want to hurt them. It's the only thing they can hold on to. A ripple goes through the crowd, and the dead move into formation. With the creak of age-old bones and the rip of torn muscles, they start to walk, a strange macabre parade down the street, heading east, toward the morning sun.

"You didn't tell me," Adam says after they've been walking for a few minutes. The smell is choking, impossible to get used to, and they're both breathing heavily through their mouths. "You didn't tell me you nearly died getting the tattoo for me. To protect me. That that's why you have all the others. Did I—why did you do that for me?"

"Zeke told you how I reacted badly to it," Tao says. "Zeke told me how my power was linked to who I was, that trying to destroy it would destroy me first. He saved me, stopped the metaphorical bleeding. She really did nearly kill me, without even meaning to. It felt—it felt exactly like how I always imagined dying would feel. Painful. Suffocating. Helpless. And Zeke saved me. I know it's ugly, that they're ugly, but I can't—it doesn't feel like it matters anymore, you know? Everything feels less important now."

"No, I understand. It's just… you could have told me. I'm just, sorry it happened to you. I don't know. I don't understand the complexities of protective magic. It just looked like a lot. It *is* a lot. But it's keeping you safe, right? Keeping her from hurting you, even now. Gods, Tao. You did that for me. You did that for me and still thought you could be dangerous. You're ridiculous," Adam says, and there's almost a faint smile.

"Look around you," Tao says. "This doesn't feel dangerous?"

"I don't think I'm processing it right now. Does that make sense? I think afterwards, when we win this, I'll probably cry for a week. But right now I just need to keep you safe. That's what I'm focused on. Everything else feels like static. It's annoying, and it's distracting, but it's not what I'm looking at. I'm looking at you." Adam squeezes Tao's hand and sends a pulse of power that vibrates through Tao's veins.

"It feels like you can control it better now," Tao says.

"Yeah. I think—you woke it up. I can feel it. For the first time. I can feel—it's like I've been missing a sense all my life and now I have it, and it's like, oh, of course. But you've been sending it back to me. Don't think I haven't noticed. Do you think—I don't know. It seems like we were meant to meet, you know? We have these powers, and they—they like each other. That's something, right?"

Adam keeps walking but bumps his shoulder against Tao's. Tao bumps back.

"When this is all over and when I've cried for a week, what do you say to getting coffee?" Adam aims for nonchalant and just misses.

Tao barks out a small laugh despite everything.

"Yeah, I think I'd like that," they say.

"You'll still want me around?" Adam asks.

"I'll still want you around," Tao says softly.

"I'm glad." Adam bumps Tao's shoulder again and sends a wave of power over to Tao that leaves them tingling and warm.

They're approaching the outskirts of the city now, and Tao is pretty sure they know where they're headed. They keep walking in formation, the dead all around them, leading them, but it's becoming clearer. There was only one place this could really end, wasn't there?

"Does she know what I am?" Adam asks. "I mean—I don't want to worry about myself right now because I'm too busy worrying about you. And this is still me worrying about you. If she's as powerful as Zeke seems to think, then she could use me, right? What if—what if she tries to use me against you?"

"Won't happen," Tao says, certain of this at least. "It just won't. I don't think she even knows. You didn't know. I didn't know. She never paid any attention to you when you were in the studio. Just said you had weird vibes. She's—she—I guess, I guess it makes sense now. She was always quick to dismiss people, and I thought she just had high standards, you know, making snarky comments and that. I thought that was just how she was, but now, it was about power, wasn't it? You didn't have that. She didn't look at you twice. Didn't care to look. So I don't think she knows."

"I don't want to be—one of—" Adam gestures to the dead around them. "—one of them. I don't want to be empty. If that happens to me, you'll—what you did to Luis, right? Gods, I'm asking you this like it's something I'm even allowed to ask of you. There's already so much, and I'm asking more."

"She won't do that to you. I won't let her. I promise. No matter what happens, I won't let her touch you," Tao says, fierce and loyal and true. They'd rather die than see Adam become an empty husk of a thing. There's no way they'd allow that to happen. They love Pru, but they'd kill her with their bare hands before they let her hurt Adam.

"She's your friend first," Adam says. "I'm just… somebody. I'm just here."

"She's my friend, was my friend. I don't know. I'm not going to argue semantics right now. But you're—you're my…." Tao pauses and thinks for a few seconds, trying to put it into words. "You're the future I want to walk toward. You're the thing pulling me through this right now, okay? When it's all over, I'm going to need you there. So I'm going to do everything to make sure that happens." Tao sends waves of power through their connection, everything they can't put into words.

"I trust you," Adam says—three words that sound like he could be saying something else, something more. "I really do. I want you to know that. I always have. Always will."

"We're going to go out for coffee." Tao stops walking because the cemetery gates are in sight now and the dead have slowed their pace. Adam stops walking too, and Tao stares at him, turns their entire body to mirror his. Then they lean up and kiss Adam, their fingers grasping at his hair, almost but not quite painfully, and pull him as close as they can to savor every second of this touch. The sun is still barely up—only a sliver on the horizon—but Tao can feel daylight coursing through them, sunshine yellow and warm and alive. Adam gives them everything, kisses back and nips at their lips. He opens his mouth and lets their tongues move together, tastes the stale breath of a long night, until his hands come to rest on Tao's hips.

Tao pulls away, panting slightly, and looks at how red Adam's mouth is, almost bruised.

"What was that for?" Adam runs his fingers over Tao's tattoos, and Tao wonders if this is something he'll always do, lighting each one up under his touch.

"Good luck," Tao says.

"We don't need it," Adam replies. "You're you, and I'm me. We're outside a cemetery, surrounded by dead people. Why would we need luck?"

There's a screech overhead, and they both look up. A dragon loops in the air above them, all loose scales and torn-apart wings. Tao can just make out those misty white eyes.

"She has a dragon," Adam remarks mildly, beyond fear, into a strange place beyond it that is just calm acceptance. "Dragons don't exist."

Tao thinks back to the talk with Zeke—that remark that stuck with them—*one wonders*. They wonder how much Zeke has seen in his long life. How much he truly knows. They're glad, at least, that he's the backup plan.

"Apparently they do," Tao says. The dragon swoops low over their heads and then climbs again. It lets out a burst of blue flame, which wavers in the air and then dissolves.

Adam makes a small distressed noise.

"Tao," he says, staring up at the dragon, watching its movements. "Tao, dragon flame isn't man-made."

"Oh," Tao says, understanding immediately. The dead around them ripple and begin to part, and Tao can see Pru making her way toward them, her skin pale and her eyes so bruised from lack of sleep she looks like she's been in a fight.

Tao remembers the dreams, the fire that looked like it should be cold but wasn't. There it is. This is really, really it. This is the culmination.

An ending.

"She can kill you," Adam says quietly, carefully so Pru doesn't overhear, even though Tao's sure she knows. Knowledge is power too, after all. There's no reason she couldn't know this.

"It's going to be okay," Tao says, remembering Adam saying those very same words to them. "It has to be."

The dead have moved to flank Pru now, and she walks with them like it's the most natural thing in the world instead of the abomination it is. They shamble gracelessly around her.

"Little sibling," she says when they're close enough. "You came. And you brought your boyfriend. Adam, right? We haven't been introduced. I'm Pru." She gestures around the cemetery. "This is the beginning of everything."

The dragon roars above them, rusty and awful, and Pru smiles that quirked smile that never comes out quite right.

"What are you doing, Pru?" Tao asks, dreading the answer, because it can't be anything good. It won't be. It's just—they have to know.

Pru smiles wider, and the dead around her smile too, and Tao hears Adam take a shaky breath. Tao takes a step forward so Adam is behind them, but Adam reaches out to take Tao's hand and holds it between them both like a lifeline.

"Everybody's going to live forever, little sibling. I'm going to change the world."

CHAPTER NINETEEN

TAO DOESN'T know what to say to that, can't find a response. But Pru doesn't look like she expects one. It's grandiose enough that it should inspire awe, after all, which is probably what she was going for.

"Where's Zeke?" she asks, looking around past Adam, to the gates beyond. "I thought he'd be here by now."

"He's not coming," Tao manages. Something akin to disappointment flickers across Pru's face.

"Oh," she says, and the dead around her seem to slump a little. "I see. Right, well, that's hardly a surprise, is it?"

She says this bitterly, as though she expected it. As though it's some kind of personal slight on her and all she's trying to do.

"Your boyfriend bothered to turn up, but the man I've worked for for five years, the man who told me to be the best I could be, the man who gave the godsdamned inspiration for all of this, he doesn't bother to show." She pauses and looks at Tao, shakes her head. "Typical. He'd have shown for you."

"Pru," Tao says, confused. "Pru, I don't know what you mean. I don't know what you're doing. I don't know if you know what you're doing. Explain it to me, please, because I don't know what's going on."

"Little sibling, I told you, I'm going to change the world. No more death. Everybody gets to live forever. Isn't that great?" Pru says as though it all makes sense. Maybe to her it does.

Tao looks at the dead around her, the way they move as one unit, like they share the same hive mind. It must be easier for her to control them that way. Then they look up at the dragon, which flies in lazy circles, over and over. She's expending a lot of energy on this performance, and it shows.

"Pru, these… people, they're not alive. They'll never be alive again. You *killed* some of them. They're dead, Pru. Can't you see that? There's nothing to them. They're just bodies," Tao says, desperate. Pru's face contorts as they speak.

"Can't you hear them?" she asks, voice louder now, angry. "Can't you hear them talking? Begging? They've been so afraid for so long, in the dark, and I've set them free. And now look at them." She gestures to the ramshackle dozens around her as though it's something to be proud of. "They're back. And they're *singing*."

She really believes this. Whatever the blood magic did to her, there's no dishonesty in her voice. She's clear, and she doesn't trip over her words. She really, truly believes that these things are alive. That she's given them that.

"They're not singing, Pru," Tao says, feeling suddenly very tired. "They're not saying anything. They can't."

Pru cocks her head to the side, and the dead around her imitate the gesture.

"You can't hear them, can you? That's why you're so upset. Why you destroyed my gift to you. You can't hear them, and that—what? Upsets you? Because they trust me and not you? Because they chose me? You swan in and expect everything to just go your way because that's how it's always gone, but for the first time, it doesn't, and you get mad at me. And Zeke didn't show, and he should be here!" She switches subjects like she's speaking every word that comes to mind, and Tao can't be surprised. All her energy is taken up by controlling the dead, making them mimic her. She can't possibly think rationally with all of that inside her head.

"Why do you think Zeke needs to be here?" Tao asks gently. "Is that important to you?"

Tao talks as though this is normal, as though they're in the studio and having a normal conversation. Maybe it'll help.

"I thought he'd like to see this," Pru says. "He always encouraged me to do my best. And here I am, doing my best. I'm trying so hard. And he isn't here, and he should be."

"He's letting you down," Tao says, and Pru nods. The dead nod with her. Tao wonders how much of them being in sync with Pru is a conscious choice for her after all.

"He's so powerful, little sibling," Pru says. "So, so powerful. And so unwilling to share. That stupid block. I came to him because

I'd heard of what he'd done, the wars he'd fought in, the battles he'd won. He's killed necromancers, you know? He's killed people just like us. People talk about him like he's a god, like he's been here forever. So of course I wanted to work for him, of course I wanted to be around him, to learn from him. And he treated me like an equal. From day one, he always treated me like an equal. Encouraged me. Told me to leave the world a better place than I found it. Well, here it is, and he's not here to see it! Why isn't he here, little sibling?" The last sentence comes out softer, and her face is riddled with hurt.

"He'll be here soon," Tao lies, because maybe this is the answer. "He was just a bit confused by what you were doing. That's all. He thinks maybe you've made some bad choices. But it's not too late. You don't have to keep doing this."

Pru fiddles with the hem of her sweater, and the dead mimic the motion again, and they're definitely tied to her in a way that she can't completely control. Tao can see that. She may be the head, but they're the body. Tao tries not to think of decapitation.

"You said he wasn't coming," she says, confused. "Why would you lie?"

Tao thinks for a moment before replying.

"Pru, what you're doing… you do realize that the police are going to come and stop you, don't you? They'll kill you. And you won't stand back up. And if you die, all of—all of your friends will die too. All the people you've raised. Zeke doesn't want to see that. Because he cares about you. He told me, he sees so much of himself in you. Always has."

"Really?" Pru asks, and Tao can tell she's desperate to believe this. They can't help but wonder why this matters to her so much, that Zeke is here, but it seems to be something they can work with.

"Yeah. He sent me to make sure you were okay. Because it's my fau—my power that caused this. That… let you. Hear them," Tao says, nearly tripping over their words. It's hard to know what to say, because Pru is so far gone now, so lost in this fantasy. The wrong word could cause her to—they don't even know what. They just know that Adam's grip on their hand is steady and warm, the only warm thing in the world right now.

"You gave this to me," Pru agrees. "I couldn't believe it. The one thing I wanted most. And you never asked for anything, never held it above me. You just passed it on and let me have it. That's why I sent you a gift. Your friend, the one you visit so often. He was old, but I made it so he wouldn't be anymore. You could have been friends forever. Except you didn't. He's gone now. Why did you do that?"

She looks more puzzled than angry, like she really can't understand it. Tao tries not to reel about the fact that their power is the reason Luis is dead. They push it down, try to keep up the charade.

"It was a mistake," they say, lying through their teeth. "My wards went off, and I was scared. I didn't know who'd sent him to me. I didn't know it was you. I didn't know anything about you until Zeke told me. I'm sorry, Pru. It was—he was a great gift. Really. You're right, he was my friend." Adam's grip tightens. "And you did the right thing. But I think now it's time to stop, don't you? You've done so well. Look at all these... people you've got here. They're all... alive because of you. You can stop this now. It'll be okay if you stop."

"No, that's not right," Pru says, sounding confused. "If I stop, then who's going to save everybody else? You're not going to do it. You don't... you don't believe me. You're saying you do, but you don't. Little sibling, you're... you're saying things you don't think are true. You don't... you want me to stop because you're scared. But there's nothing to be scared of. Why are you scared? It's all going to be okay. I can fix everything. That's what we're designed to do. No more death. Nothing to be afraid of. They're so loud in my head, little sibling. So happy. I did that. Why can't you hear them? Why isn't Zeke here?"

It's like her brain can't focus on something for more than a few seconds. Tao looks up at the dragon, and the lazy circles are becoming erratic. It flies like it can barely hold itself up in the sky. She's using so much power, so much energy it's breaking her apart.

"Pru, just focus on me," Tao tries. "Just focus on me right now. Tell me why this is so important to you. Tell me why you don't want anyone to die."

She scoffs, wrinkles her nose, and the dead around her that still have noses do it too. It's awful.

"That's silly, little sibling. Why wouldn't I do this? If you could, you *can*, stop death. Why aren't you? Why haven't you been? Why did you wait for me? Is it because you've never lost anyone? Is that it, little sibling? You don't know, do you? How much it burns inside of you? The ache you can't get rid of? The way you want to tear yourself apart and pull it out of you just to feel something other than that loss? You don't know it at all, do you?"

Tao thinks about Luis, about that first second of realization. That he was gone. That he was gone and some dead thing was wearing his face.

But no. Until tonight they hadn't felt that before. They've been lucky. They haven't been close enough to anybody to lose them.

But Pru has. Pru has lost somebody. Somebody important. This is why she's doing it. Why she's doing all of it. It makes sense now. She's trying to fix things.

Zeke said she'd always been power hungry. How long has she been looking for this?

"Who did you lose, Pru?" Tao asks softly. "You can tell me."

"Now you ask." Pru tries to smile but fails. "Three years and you finally ask. I thought you never would. So wrapped up in your own world. So afraid of yourself, like a scorpion afraid of its own sting, that you never asked how anybody else was doing. Never asked why my grandparents raised me. Never even knew that, did you? Do you really want to know?"

"I do," Tao says. A promise. Honest. The least they can do.

"My parents are dead," Pru says and sniffs, trying to hold back tears. "When I was—I was three years old. I'd been staying at my grandparents' house because my parents wanted a break. Just a couple of days. They went camping. It rained the whole weekend. They should have been so mad. But they... they were the type of people who wouldn't have minded, not really. They'd have grumbled, but they would have made the best of it. They always did." She pauses and wipes at her cheeks, and the dead copy her once again. "They were driving back to pick me up. They phoned from the gas station that they were coming back early because they missed me. It was their first holiday since I was born, and so they were coming back early for me. My grandparents—they lived in the countryside. The roads, they were pretty narrow. Sharp corners. It was still so wet. It was dark when they set off. They wanted to be there when I woke up."

She lets out a long breath. The dead try to do the same with lungs that don't work, instead letting out a dreadful moan. Adam shivers behind Tao, and Tao feels it in their bones.

"They hit a deer," Pru continues. "Apparently they swerved to avoid it, but it was too slippery. They hit it, and the car flipped. Over and over and over. It didn't have—it was an old car. Didn't have the protective charms they have nowadays. They were trapped inside, and it was still dark. And then the engine caught fire."

Now Tao understands why Pru latched on to Zeke, why she wanted him here so badly. Her desperate need to raise the dead. They don't have time to think anymore because she's still talking—

"The reports say they died of smoke inhalation. But they're just being kind, aren't they? They burned alive, trapped there, watching the fire creep closer. What do you do when the person you love is going to burn? When there's nothing you can do but sit and watch because you're going to burn too? Do you think they hated me in that moment? They'd only been on that bit of road at that particular moment in time because of me. Because they wanted to surprise me. I killed them." Pru is sobbing openly now, and Tao tries not to look at the dead around her, the hollow mimicry of mourning. "The fire burned for three hours before anyone else drove past. Three hours and nobody knew they were dead. I didn't understand. My grandparents told me that my parents weren't coming, and I didn't understand."

She pauses, blinking hard, taking deep breaths.

"Are they here?" Tao asks, though none of the dead she's raised look like they died in a fire.

She shakes her head.

"My grandparents had them cremated. They're gone. I can't—I can't find them. There's nothing left of them. I can't save them. I can't bring them back. Little sibling, do you know how it feels to have this power and not be able to use it on the people who matter to you the most? Do you understand? Nobody should have to feel that way. Nobody. So I'm going to make sure nobody ever does. I'm going to bring them all back. And then, I'm going to save the rest of the world."

She lowers herself to her knees and digs her hands into the earth. Tao knows what she's going to do before she does it but doesn't know how to stop her. They can only watch. The dead are kneeling too, and it seems like some unholy ritual.

The ground trembles around them, and Tao can feel the tendrils of Pru's power reaching out to all the bodies that rest there.

"She's going to raise the whole cemetery," they breathe, horrified.

Overhead, the dragon lets out an agonized roar.

Pru looks up at Tao and smiles.

"Help me, little sibling." She tilts her head, confused. "Why aren't you helping me?"

CHAPTER TWENTY

"THAT'S ENOUGH!" Adam cries out from behind Tao, and it seems to jolt Pru. She looks up at him sharply, and Tao feels the tendrils of her power withdrawing from the earth.

"I'd forgotten you were here," she says, seemingly confused.

"Yeah, that'll happen," Adam replies. "Raising the dead can be distracting."

"Adam, stop," Tao says. "Pru—Pru, you've got to stop too. This is enough. It's enough now."

"What, because your boyfriend says so?" Pru asks and scoffs. "You really care about him, don't you? You know you'll outlive him, right? He'll grow old, and you won't. And he'll resent you for that, every single day. Maybe not at first, but it's inevitable. And one day, one day he's going to die. Tell me you won't bring him back. Can you tell me you won't? Or are you a hypocrite?"

Adam's bought them some much-needed time by distracting Pru, but now she's single-minded, needling away at Tao as though she can make them believe what she believes.

"You know I never would, never could," Tao says.

"Do you want me to do it for you?" Pru asks, and it's a genuine offer, kindness in her voice despite everything that's been said and done. "If you can't do it, I can do it. He can be young forever. You get to keep him forever. That's what you want, isn't it?"

She stands and takes a step toward them. Tao raises the hand not holding Adam's to warn her off.

"Don't touch him," they say.

"It's so quick, little sibling, so quick. He won't feel it. And then he'll be back. And he'll sing. Just like the others. Just like Luis." She steps forward again.

Tao squeezes Adam's hand and feels a burst of power jump from skin to skin. They focus it toward Pru and blast her backward, causing her to skid and fall forward, scrape her palms on the earth, hit her face in the dirt and come up bloodied. Around her, the dead fall haphazardly, like their strings have been cut. It'd be farcical under any other circumstance. She shakily gathers herself to her feet.

"What the hell, Tao?" she asks, voice full of venom.

"Pru, you have to stop. Don't make me make you. I'm begging you. You're sick. I can get you help. Zeke must know somebody. There's got to be another way," Tao begs.

"No," Pru says. "No, I don't think so. Zeke kills our kind. That's what he does. That's what they all do. They don't understand. Gods, nobody seems to understand what I'm trying to do here!"

"Because it doesn't make sense! I'm sorry about your parents. I'm so gods damn sorry. But this won't bring them back. This won't fix anything. I know you think it will, but it can't. Nothing can. They're dead, Pru," Tao says, because they're so tired and because they're just going around in circles.

"You don't want to understand," Pru fires back. "You're not trying. You should be helping me. You gave me this power. You made me this. This is what we're built to do. Use it, little sibling. Stop being so afraid of yourself, of what you can do."

"I can't. I can't do that. You know I can't." Tao lowers their hand. They look at Pru—the grayish tint to her skin, the way her lips are cracked open, her blue eyes dulled with exhaustion. "This is killing you, Pru. You're not built for this. Maybe I am, but you're not. It's borrowed power. It's too much. It's not sustainable."

"You won't hurt me," Pru says. "Whatever you say, you won't hurt me. That's why you came here, not Zeke. Because you knew you would never actually stop me. You might be the only person in the world who could, you know? But you won't do it. And I wouldn't do it to you. We're siblings. A rare species. So let me do this, little sibling. Let me stop all the pain, all the suffering, all the heartache. Let me bring them all back. You can keep him"—she gestures to Adam—"until you realize. What does he have, fifty years? That's nothing. He could have forever. Don't be selfish, little sibling. Let yourself fly."

She lowers herself to the ground again, the dead around her. Tao feels the tendrils of her power reaching out again, into the earth, sparking awake something inside the dead. The earth rumbles its disapproval.

"Adam," Tao murmurs. A small spark of power zips through in a reply.

Tao looks up at the dragon, still stuck in its uneven loop, then at the dead surrounding Pru, then at the ground beneath their feet. They look inside themself and find the power there, raw and waiting. They close their eyes and drop Adam's hand. Adam immediately moves to place both hands between Tao's shoulder blades.

Power bursts forth, firing through Tao's veins like a shot of adrenaline—life, untamed and wild. They aim one hand at the dragon, the other at the semicircle of dead. They close their eyes and reach out, following the inky strings that tie them all together in the darkness.

They—they're above everything. Their eyes are still closed, but they can see everything—every connection, every ember. The dragon looms large in their vision, flaming bright, and they wish it away, cutting the strings that hold it up, hand shooting out to direct the power that flows from them into the sky.

With their other hand, they move to disentangle the strings that tie the dead to Pru. It's a different kind of complicated, and it feels like it takes an age. They fall, one by one, and disintegrate just like Luis did, into nothing. The embers die out, one by one, behind closed eyelids.

The dragon turns to ash and, like snowflakes, powders down to the ground around them.

Somewhere, a long way away, Tao can hear Pru screaming.

She's fighting back with everything she's got, but she's exhausted, and Tao can feel it, feel the way the power is slipping away from her, out of her control, its grasp loosening on the dead, on her.

Adam shudders behind them, and they both fall to their knees, Adam resting his head between Tao's shoulder blades, still sending as much power as he can and then still more. Tao can feel that effort now, the strain of it, and they shake with it, narrowing their focus to the earth, where hundreds, thousands of bodies are awakening.

There's no hive mind here; Pru is panicking, and it shows. Each one sparks into existence at random, and Tao snuffs it out just as readily, and on, and on, and on it goes—Pru screaming and screaming and Tao cutting every single tie as soon as it's knotted to her. It goes on forever. Powers collide and mix until there's no end or beginning, only the fight, and Tao doesn't open their eyes, because it's not done, not yet.

They have to do this, have to end it. Have to cut out the rot.

Tao reaches out for Pru, and gods, how she shines, so much brighter than the rest in the darkness. Tao wraps around her power, that borrowed power, and pulls, trying to tug it free from her. They know what'll happen. They know what they're doing. They know how it felt. There's no way to perform a clean amputation. They have to do this. Behind them, Adam is letting out desperate sobs, clinging painfully to Tao, and still Pru screams.

Something in Pru's power recognizes Tao, recognizes where it came from and where it was born. Tao pulls harder at it, wraps it around themself, urges it home. It ekes away from her, drop by stubborn drop, a waterfall in slow motion, until Tao is drowning by degrees.

It stretches like an elastic, taut between them, loosening, letting go, and then—

It snaps. Tao falls backward, falls into Adam, who stumbles, lets go of Tao, and scrambles to find a new hold. Pru's power sits heavy and itchy inside Tao for a long minute, unsettled, searching for belonging, and Tao keeps their eyes closed, urging it to calm, to find peace, to find the familiarity of where it came from.

They feel Adam grip their hand and pull them to a sitting position. They hold on, fighting the power down, fighting to keep it inside.

Pru isn't screaming anymore.

The flood recedes like the tide, and Tao is left standing in the shallows, gasping for air. The power settles and becomes one with their own again.

Tao opens their eyes.

Everything is covered with a fine layer of ash. It falls from the sky like winter snow, coating everything it touches. Pru lies folded on the ground, one hand desperately clutching at the dirt, barely breathing.

Tao shifts to find Adam taking huge gulping breaths like he too was drowning.

Tao's hands find Adam's cheeks, smearing the ash upon them, find his hair, find the nape of his neck. Tao pulls him close and presses their face to his throat, nose against pulse, opens the doors to their power again and lets it flow back to Adam, filling him with all that had been returned to them, allowing him the chance to catch his breath, to fill his lungs.

They don't know anything else but Adam for a long moment.

Adam breathes Tao in and clutches tightly to Tao's back, digging in fingernails that scratch even through Tao's sweater. Tao allows the hurt, allows the wet of tears as Adam cries because Tao is crying too, and Tao is holding on just as hard.

"Is it over?" Adam asks, voice shaky. "Is it done?"

Tao doesn't want to turn to look at Pru, doesn't want to look at what they've done to her. They remember too clearly how it felt on that tattoo bench, what dying felt like. She did that to them. And now they've repaid the favor.

It doesn't feel like winning. It feels like losing a friend.

"Is she okay?" Adam asks. He doesn't know what Tao's done. Doesn't know the extent of it yet. Gods.

Tao shakes their head against Adam's neck.

"No," they say. "She's not okay. She's not going to be okay."

Adam is silent for a few seconds.

"What about you? Are you okay?" he asks and holds Tao a little tighter.

"No," they reply. "I—I know I had to. I had to do it. But I didn't want to. I never wanted to. I didn't—I don't remember making the choice to do it. I just knew I had to. She was never going to stop, was she? We could have tried to talk to her forever and she'd never have listened. I took it. I took it all. The power she took from me. I gave it to you. It belongs to both of us now. I don't know what that means, but it—it's like instinct. Everything was so dark, and all I could see were the little lights she was trying to turn on. And I had to turn them off. But she was—there was so much to her. And I took it all. Gods, I took it all."

"It's okay," Adam says. He brushes his hand through Tao's hair and strokes down to the tattoos on their forehead. "It's okay now."

"She's dying," Tao says softly. "I did that."

"You saved so many people," Adam replies. "You—the dragon. You took down a dragon. That was pretty impressive."

"I hurt you," Tao says, because they must have. "The power it took to hold the dragon. To hold the dead back. I took so much from you. How much—I'm sorry. I'm so sorry."

"It's okay," Adam repeats. "You did what you had to do. I knew—well, no, but I was prepared for… worse. You could have taken everything and I'd have forgiven you. To stop her. To save the city. This is our home, Tao, and you saved it. You did it."

Behind them, Pru lets out a small moan, barely there.

"You should go to her," Adam says. "Nobody should die alone."

"I'm scared," Tao says. "I don't want to do this."

Adam tilts Tao's chin up and presses their foreheads together, noses nudging against one another.

"I know you don't owe her anything, but you owe it to yourself to do this. She was your friend. Go to her."

On shaking, stumbling legs, Tao crosses the distance, boots dragging in the ash, and goes to their friend.

Chapter Twenty-One

IT's LESS than one hundred feet, but it seems to take an age to cross the distance. Pru doesn't move except for her hand, clenching at the dirt, and Tao watches as it seeps through the gaps between her fingers. They can't do this.

They have to.

"Pru." Tao kneels and pulls her to them, her head in their lap. They brush the ash from her cheeks, from the blond of her hair. She feels like she weighs nothing, like she could float away at any second. She's barely breathing, barely there at all. It's hard to reconcile with the powerhouse she was minutes before. Now she feels almost empty.

"Little sibling," she says, barely more than a whisper, and the words catch in her throat. "You're here."

"Couldn't be anywhere else," Tao says. They find her hand and hold it gently, lacing their fingers between hers. Her pulse is so weak now, like every heartbeat could be her last.

She's dying.

Tao did this to her.

A flurry of ash falls, and Tao leans over to protect her, to shield her face. She looks up at them, her eyelids heavy.

"Is it over?" she asks.

"Yeah," they say. It's over now. It's all over. The dead are dead again, and Pru is dying, and it's over.

"I'm not sorry," she says and coughs a little, struggling to breathe. "I know you want me to be sorry, but I'm not. You understand, don't you? Please tell me you understand."

"I do, Pru. I do. You just wanted to save people. That's—that's not a bad thing. Just, maybe you went about it the wrong way," Tao says, and Pru gives them a watery smile.

"I can—I can think clearly now. Like there was this fog. But it's gone now. I've been so lost," she says, and it ends with a small sob.

"I know, I know. It's okay now. It's all going to be okay," Tao says—a lie, because it can't be. It won't be. Not for her.

Maybe not for either of them.

"I'm scared," Pru says in a small voice. "I'm so scared."

"Me too," Tao says and holds her hand a little tighter. "But it's okay. You're allowed to be scared. Pru, you were so powerful. I could see it. You shone so bright. You always did. Always will."

"Do you think it matters, in the end?" she asks. "Power? Do you think it matters? I always thought it did. But now… now I'm not so sure."

"Maybe it's about what you do with it," Tao says carefully. "It's the choices we make. Every day."

"You think I made bad ones." Pru closes her eyes for a second. "Maybe I did. Do you think… do you think they'll forgive me? The people I hurt? Do you think you'll forgive me, one day?"

Her breathing stutters, and her chest rises and falls unevenly.

"In time," Tao says, holding on so tightly now, not wanting her to go. Not ready for goodbye, not yet.

"You have so much time, little sibling. So much. More than most," Pru says, looking up at them with those faded blue eyes. "You're going to be amazing. You and—you and your boy, you're going to be magnificent."

Tao glances back at Adam, who has taken a few steps closer to them. He hangs back, watching, chewing nervously on his lip. There's ash in his hair and smeared across his glasses. His coat is speckled with it. He's still the most beautiful thing Tao has ever seen.

"You were magnificent," Tao says as they turn back to Pru. "Terrible perhaps, but magnificent."

"What a way to be remembered." Pru smiles a small version of her crooked smile. "Terrible but magnificent. I like that."

"You will be," Tao says, "remembered. For so long. I'll make sure of it. Not for this, but for everyone you helped protect. For being the best big sister a person could ask for." Their voice breaks now and they hold back tears. They don't want her to see them cry. They don't want to make this harder for her.

"Don't bring me back, little sibling," she says. "Promise me that. You won't bring me back."

"Never," Tao promises. "I would never do that."

"I know," Pru says. "I just—I'm so scared. Of the dark. When you—when you took it. When you took it all, it got so dark. I couldn't hear them anymore. It was just me again. It's always been just me. I don't want to be on my own again in the dark."

She's sobbing now in tiny little gasps, and Tao can't stop the tears from falling and wipes at them with their spare hand.

"You won't be alone," they promise nervously, a lie, the truth, they don't know anymore. "You won't be. There are so many people waiting for you. Think about your parents. They must have missed you so much."

Pru blinks up at Tao, eyes wide.

"Do you think they'll be there?" she asks, sounding like the child she was all those years ago.

"They'll be there," Tao says, because lying is easy right now. It's the easiest thing in the world. It's comfort, cold comfort, and Pru needs to hear it. It's all they can give her.

"And they won't be angry with me?" she asks, and she's so frag-ile, so barely there, her voice so small. Her fear is so present.

"Why would they be angry? Pru, you're their daughter. Nothing you could do—nothing you could ever do will change that," Tao says, thinking of their own parents. Pru was loved in a way they had never been. Loved so much. They have no doubt that her parents would forgive her anything.

"I've been waiting for them," she says, and it's more of a sigh now. "I've been waiting every day since that morning, since I woke up and they weren't there. I barely remember them, but I know how to miss them. That's all I've ever known—how much I've missed them."

"You'll see them soon," Tao says. "You don't have to be scared. It's okay. They're waiting."

"Will you—my grandparents. Can you get me home to my grandparents? I don't want—I don't want to be so far away. I want to go home," she says, and Tao nods.

In the distance, sirens ring out—police sirens—and Tao knows time is running out for both of them now.

"I'll get you home. I'll make sure of it," Tao promises.

"Don't tell them what I did," Pru says. Then she coughs, her chest wracked with it. "Don't tell them."

"I won't," Tao says.

"Tao," Adam says from behind them. "The police are coming."

"It'll hurt like hell," Pru says, and using all her strength, she lifts her hand to Tao's face and pushes a finger against their forehead. "It'll hurt like hell, but you'll survive it if you want to."

"Pru—" Tao starts.

"I'm really tired. It's getting so late," Pru says, though the sun is up now, pale yellow across the empty cemetery, illuminating the still-falling ash. "If I go to sleep, will you be here when I wake up?" she asks.

"Yeah." Tao chokes up and listens to the sirens getting louder and louder. They hold her tighter, and her arm falls down beside her like she's a rag doll. "I'll be right here."

"I think I'm going to sleep," she says, eyes closing. "Good night, little sibling. *Tao*. See you in the morning."

"See you in the morning," Tao echoes, and Pru's eyes slip closed, her mouth parting slightly as she inhales, exhales, and then stops. It's a slow slipping away that leaves her body limp and heavy in Tao's arms.

"Tao, we need to leave." Adam puts a hand on Tao's shoulder.

"I can't leave her," Tao says, holding on to the—the body that was Pru. "I promised her I'd get her to her grandparents. I can't leave her."

The sirens stop wailing, and Tao can make out the sound of heavy footsteps and shouting.

"Tao!" Adam cries out, desperate.

Tao can't do it, can't leave Pru behind. They wipe away the ash from her eyelashes, smooth her hair. Wherever she is now, if she's anywhere, they hope she's okay.

"Put your hands behind your head and step away from the girl!" a voice shouts, male and angry, full of barely contained disgust.

Tao doesn't move, doesn't turn.

"Tao, please," Adam begs, but he sounds very far away.

"Put your godsdamned hands up and get away from her!" The voice says, closer now. There's the sound of guns being readied.

Tao gently lowers Pru's body to the ground, puts their hands behind their head, and gets shakily to their feet. They look at her—peaceful now—and turn slowly.

Adam stands a few feet away, flickering in and out of existence, causing Tao's eyes to dart wildly as they try to focus on him. The police officers don't seem to have noticed him, or if they have, they don't care. *The incredible disappearing boy.* Even to the end.

They care about Tao, though, and Tao has never seen so many guns. The police officer who shouted moves closer, the gun in his hand trembling as he aims it at Tao's face.

"Get on your knees," he shouts. Tao looks at Adam's pain-stricken blurring face. "Look at me, vermin, and get on your godsdamned knees!"

Tao lowers themself to the ground again and kneels in the ash there. The police officer takes another step forward and pushes the barrel of the gun against Tao's forehead, hard enough to bruise. Tao tries to lean away from it. They look up at this man, at his fear, and wonder what he sees.

"Godsdamned necromancers make me sick to my stomach," the officer spits, and his gun shakes a little, losing contact with Tao's skin and waving past their left eye instead. "Ain't nothing sacred to you, huh? Godsdamned freaks. Gotta mess with the dead. Guess what? That's you. For what you did to that girl. You'll be in the ground too. Ain't nobody going to be mourning you."

Tao looks past the officer and at Adam, and smiles. If this is the last thing they see, the last thing they get to see, they want to choose Adam.

"Tao," Adam says, like a whisper on the wind.

"It's okay." Tao looks up at the sky, at the fluff of clouds above them. It's morning. The darkness is gone.

"What the hell are you talking about?" the cop asks as he shifts his grip on the gun and points it closer to Tao's eye, hand shaking violently.

"It's okay," Tao repeats, finding Adam, speaking to Adam, speaking to—the whole damn universe. They close their eyes.

"Freak," the officer spits. "Nothing but a godsdamned freak."

The gun cocks, and Tao tries not to flinch. The police officer shouts back, asking for—asking for permission. *Gods.*

Tao wonders vaguely what'll become of this man, because spilled blood is spilled blood.

The irony isn't lost on them that he'll become the thing he hates most.

Tao hopes Zeke will be there to clean up the mess.

It'll hurt like hell, Pru had said.

But you'll survive it.

If you want to.

Tao wants to survive—wants to see another day with Adam, wants to get Pru home to her grandparents, wants an entire long life, well lived and happy. Unafraid. Safe.

Shouts of confirmation from the other officers echo back, and Tao can hear Adam sobbing in the breeze.

In the end, Pru was right. The police officer shifts his grip again and fires.

It hurts like hell.

Tao pitches forward, and the dirt catches them and crushes up into their open mouth. It tastes of ash.

It was always going to end like this.

The darkness reaches out to them, and they sink into it willingly.

CHAPTER TWENTY-TWO

TAO DOESN'T dream. They sink into the darkness and far away from the hurt. They're aware of nothing but the darkness and the way it clings to them, keeping them safe. There's nobody and nothing, and they're not even really there themself. They exist, but only to witness the black emptiness that allows them sanctuary.

THE FIRST time Tao wakes up, the room is dimly lit but still far too bright. They force their eyes open and try to look around, but they can't—can't see properly—and gods, their head hurts. It's like someone is driving coffin nails into their skull. They flinch to try to get away from it. A hand finds theirs, and they can make out a voice they recognize but can't place. It's soothing. Far away. A second voice, lyrical, softer, joins it, and a hand brushes against their forehead. For a few seconds the pain eases. A spark of power flows through them, and with it, warmth and love. They know they should try to stay awake, but the voices are so far away, and the darkness is getting closer again. That small piece of warmth is lulling them back to sleep, calming them and slowing their heartbeat. They close their eyes again. and the voices don't follow.

THE SECOND time? Third? They're not sure. When they wake up again, their head still pounds, but it's not the grinding sharpness of before. They open their eyes, and daylight seeps in through curtained windows. They still can't see properly; it's like the darkness won't leave them entirely. It encroaches on the side of their vision, and they can't blink it away. They manage to move their head and hiss with pain as they jostle it, and—there's a hand already on theirs, loosely but there. It tightens and there's Adam, Adam leaning into view. Adam who looks so tired and like he's been crying for days. Maybe he has been.

"You're awake," he says, and it sounds like he's speaking from under water. Tao tries to speak, but they can't quite find the words. Everything's jumbled, slightly broken. They try to nod instead, but that hurts too, and Adam hushes them and sends another wave of warmth through to them. And it was him before, but not just him. There's somebody else here, somebody new.

Tao has so many questions, but they're all mixed up and fragmented, and they can't think properly.

"Go back to sleep, Tao," Adam says. "I'll be here when you wake up."

That seems somehow familiar to Tao, but they can't place it. It's comforting at least. They let their eyes fall shut again and manage to squeeze Adam's hand back, ever so gently.

TAO LOSES track of time, wakes up, falls back to sleep for a few seconds but then for minutes. Adam is there every time, and sometimes somebody else—a woman. Tao has realized that she's a healer and that she is kind, and that her magic and Adam's are mixing and flowing through Tao's veins and making them well again. They can't find the words still, and the pain is dull and repetitive, a thudding metronome. They don't want to stay awake, not really, not yet. They'll sleep a little longer, just a little longer.

WHEN THEY wake up properly, the world makes a little more sense. They can think coherently, and when they open their eyes, the darkness is still there. It fuzzes the side of their vision, but they can see around it and make more sense out of what they're seeing. They turn their head, ignoring the pain that still roars when they do it, and find Adam, hunched over the side of the bed, his hand on theirs and his hair a mess. He must have fallen asleep where he sat. Tao doesn't want to wake him, but Adam seems to know and lifts his head. He sits up slowly and leans back in the chair but never lets go of Tao's hand.

He uses his other hand to rub at his eyes, which are red-rimmed and bruised from crying and lack of sleep.

"Are you really here this time?" he asks. "You've woken up a lot, but you seem to forget every time. Are you here now?"

Tao tries to sit up, but Adam sees what they're doing and moves his hand to their arm.

"Easy. Not yet. Take it slow."

Tao wants to argue, and words run like honey through their brain—legible but slow.

"How long?" they ask. "Asleep?"

"Seven days," Adam replies. "Since it happened. Since... everything. You've been asleep for most of it. There was a healer—Eir—she helped you. I helped her. She said it would take time, that you might be confused. Gods, Tao, it's been a week. I wasn't sure if you'd ever wake up properly. I'm so glad you're here."

It's a lot of words, and Tao focuses hard to process them.

"Crying," they say. Adam looks confused. "You," they say, and their tongue feels so thick and unwieldy. "You're crying."

Adam presses the fingers of his spare hand to his face as though he wasn't aware of it. His smile looks small and broken.

"Yeah, that's been happening a lot lately. I was worried about you. And besides, didn't I promise you a week of crying? I might have to amend that. A week doesn't feel nearly long enough."

Tao tries to smile back, and they're not sure if they succeed. Their face feels alien to them, like all the muscles have been reset.

"Coffee," they say. They wonder if Adam remembers.

"No, no coffee for you, not yet. Not for a long time." Then he realizes. "Oh, oh yeah. Definitely. There will be coffee. I... yeah. We're still doing that. But not for a while. This—this didn't really factor into those plans. But I still want that. Yeah. You still want it too?"

"Yeah," Tao says, and Adam smiles wider. This is the boy they were walking toward, and it still is. And now everything is—is it over? Is it finally over? Where are they? "Where?" They move their eyes to look around the room.

"My apartment," Adam says. "They—they ransacked yours. The police. Looking for—what, I don't know. Evidence? I went there while Zeke was with you. Do you remember Zeke being here? No?

That's okay. Zeke looked after you for about an hour or so, and I ran over because I remembered—do you remember Luis?" It must show on Tao's face that of course they do, and that pain hits them afresh. "Sorry, of course you do. Eir said you might have some memory issues at first. It's okay. I'm sorry. I didn't want to leave him there. But I didn't know how much time I had. This is—terrible. I'm so sorry. I gathered his ashes and put them in your Tupperware. Just until I knew what to do with them. I didn't have time for anything more… elegant. I've been feeling guilty about it ever since I did it."

Tao barks out a laugh that hurts, but they don't mind. The Tupperware wasn't theirs; it had been Luis's. He always sent them home with leftovers. He'd have gotten a kick out of that, they think.

"His," they say, trying to explain. "Luis. His Tup—Tup. His. Funny. Not bad."

They're still getting stuck on words, but at least they can understand them better now, can understand what Adam is telling them.

Adam stops looking so worried.

"It was his Tupperware? I put a man's ashes in his own Tupperware? Gods. Tao, this is ridiculous. It's all ridiculous."

Tao feels a wave of exhaustion hit them all at once.

"Tired," they say. They look at Adam. "You too."

"I'm okay," he says. "I've been resting." Tao can hear the lie of it, and with as much energy as they can muster, they pat the side of the bed next to them and make a demanding whine of a noise in the back of their throat.

"I don't want to hurt you," Adam says. "Your head. It's still healing. What if I hurt you?"

"Sleep." Tao puts as much force behind the word as possible. They're so tired. Will they always be tired now?

"Okay, but only for a little while." Adam lets go of Tao's hand to stand, cracking joints as he does. He moves around the bed in jerking motions like his limbs aren't properly coordinated with his brain. *He's tired too, so tired.*

As gently as he can, Adam gets into the bed beside Tao, on top of the duvet that covers Tao. He's too far away, and Tao whines despite themself. He seems to understand and moves closer. Then he rests his hand on Tao's shoulder, his body an open parenthesis that arches toward Tao.

"Better?" he asks, and Tao wants to reply, to say "Yes, so much better," but instead closes their eyes, just for a moment, just to blink away the sleep there, and falls into the darkness again.

SOMETHING HAS shifted when they wake up again, and they can feel the warmth of Adam's body, can recognize it and all the places they're touching. One of Adam's legs is thrown across theirs, his arm loose over their stomach. He's wriggled under the duvet in his sleep, and his face is open and childlike as he rests. Tao can only marvel at it.

They don't want to wake him, so they just watch him sleep, this beautiful boy who has been through so much, more than they want to think about. And they *can* think now, can think clearly, even if their vision is still an odd haze of clear and dark.

They don't know how long they stare. It could be a thousand years. Adam comes around slowly, reaches forward, and finds his hand already on Tao's stomach. He curls his fingers so his knuckles rest just above Tao's belly button.

"Hey, you," he says as he pushes himself up with his elbow to rest his head on his other hand. Tao wants to do the same, but their head still hurts too much to consider it. Instead they smile, and their face still feels oddly numb, but less so. It tingles now, as though the nerves there are waking up.

"Hey yourself," Tao replies properly, with full words.

"You're feeling better," Adam says and smiles back. Tao had forgotten the full force of that sunshine smile and how much it takes their breath away.

"You're here," they say. Then, because it matters, "Is it over now?"

Adam's face does something complicated, like he's not sure what to say or how to begin to explain it.

"It's over. Mostly," he says, sounding uncertain. "We have to— we can't stay here. We're safe for now, but we'll have to leave No-mos. That's the worst of it, really. I know this is your home and you have your whole life here, but Zeke said it'd be for the best because they know your face now. Zeke's got some money together—a car, places we can stay until we figure out what we're going to do next. But there's no rush. We have time. We have so much time, Tao. I promise. We're safe for now."

Tao thinks about leaving the city, about leaving the life they've built in Nomos, the place that has felt more like home than any other. They push aside the feeling of loss and displacement. They'll worry about it later. Adam said they have time. They'll take that time.

"Where is Zeke? Why isn't he here?" they ask instead, curious more than anything. They thought they'd have seen him by now. They think they remember Adam saying he'd been here, but they have no recollection of it.

"He—he was here. While you slept. But he's, this whole thing.... He's really—upset? It hit him harder than he expected it to, I think. He cared a lot about, you know, her." Adam pauses, clearly not wanting to say her name, not yet. "I think he feels like he failed. I kind of agree with him. He should never have put you in that position. But I won't get angry. I want to, but it won't help anything. He fetched the healer, and he's going to help us leave. I don't know if we'll see him again, or for a long time. I think—when he would look at you, when your face looked—well, he just looked… broken. When I went to your apartment, I came back, and he looked like he'd been crying. I don't know. I don't know if I'll ever understand him. I just know he got you out of that cemetery and he got you here, and I have to thank him for that, if nothing else. The police, they—I watched them, after. They said, gods, they said they'd leave you for the foxes, that that's all you were good for."

"They didn't see you," Tao checks, worried. Adam shakes his head. "Good," Tao says.

Then, "The one who—the one who did it. He spilled my blood. Is he—is he safe?"

I got shot. I got shot. I should have died. It hits them for the first time, and they try to contain a sob. Adam moves closer and rests his head carefully on Tao's collarbone.

"Zeke took care of it. Those were his words. He didn't elaborate. I didn't ask. I guess he figured he owed you that much."

Tao blinks away tears and unthinkingly tries to rub at their face.

Adam puts up a hand to stop them.

"Hey, leave your face alone. It's still healing." He guides Tao's hand down again.

There's a question Tao doesn't want to ask because they're scared. After everything, they're still scared. How is that possible? It shouldn't be, but it is.

"What do I look like?" they ask slowly, not wanting an answer, not really. "Is it bad?"

"Hey, no, Tao. Look at me. Trust me, it's not bad. The healer, Eir, she was really, really good. And I told you, I helped her. Maybe on her own she couldn't have, I don't know, but together, you look— you look like you, Tao. I promise. You look like you." Adam is fervent and honest and speaks quickly.

"Then why can't I see properly?" Tao asks finally because there's something wrong, there has to be. The darkness is still there, and if they turn their head the wrong way, they can't see Adam at all.

Adam sighs, but out of frustration, not out of sadness.

"There was only so much Eir could do. Even with me. The—the bullet went in through your eye socket, came out through the back. Missed a lot of your brain, actually, as far as we can tell. Superficial wounds are easy, but your eye—sight is so—Eir said sight is finicky. She said the idea of coming out whole from all of this was quixotic at best. That the fact you still have a face is—and I quote—a gods-damned miracle. But that—you still have an eye. It just doesn't work anymore. It might get better over time, but probably not. It's—not like your other eye. It's sort of white, all over, like all the color just faded out of it. But it doesn't look bad. Eir said you could even use a glamour and nobody would be able to tell." Adam pauses. "She said the protective charms, all those protective charms Zeke did to protect against... Pru's tattoo? They helped keep your eye safe. Even if it doesn't work anymore. They mitigated the damage. It could have been a lot worse."

"That's a lot," Tao says, not sure what else to say. "Can I see it?"

"Yeah, yeah, of course," Adam says, and rolls over on the bed to reach for something. He comes back with a small shaving mirror and holds it up. Tao doesn't look at it for a long minute, but finally makes eye contact with themself in the glass.

Adam was right; their eye is a kind of milky white. It reminds them almost of the dead, and isn't that a thought? The skin around it is bruised—shades of purple, yellow, and green. They can blink and close it, even though the skin is puffy. The tattoos around it are healed now, must have healed days ago. Or maybe Eir took care of them too. Against the tan of Tao's skin and the shock of their black hair, their eye looks at odds with their appearance but not necessarily wrong. Just at odds.

"It's strange," they say, and Adam places the mirror down again.

"Eir said to think of it as a reminder that you survived. Not many people would have," Adam says. "I know that's cold comfort, but it's not a lie."

"We both survived," Tao says, really realizing for the first time. "We made it through. Do you—are you okay? I took so much from you. I knew I had to, but still. Are you okay?"

"I'm fine," Adam says easily. "You don't—do you remember, at the end, after she went down, you poured it all back into me? You gave me so much power, Tao. Zeke thinks—he thinks I might actually have power now. Not much, like there's a germ inside me and it might grow or it might not. But he thinks, because of what you did, that I might be more like you than I was before."

Tao's stomach flips uneasily.

"I didn't give you—the necromancy?" they ask, and Adam smiles a little sadly, as though knowing that his next words will hurt.

"Yeah," he says, and Tao whimpers, because this is how it started before, and they can't lose Adam too. "Hey, it's okay. It's not like with her. I didn't spill your blood, Tao. Our powers, they're so compatible, they feed off each other. Even if you hadn't done it, I would have picked it up in time. I'm not going to start, gods, raising the dead or anything. As far as Zeke can tell, the only thing we have to worry about is me aging a lot slower and possibly gaining your empathy, picking up a few new powers. But even then I'll never be like someone who was born with magic. I promise you, I'm okay. Just means you might be stuck with me a bit longer, if you want that. You don't have to. I mean, no pressure—I wasn't implying anything—"

"I said I was walking toward you, didn't I? Well here we are, on the other side. And if you're going to be around for a long time, then good. I want you around," Tao says, so certain.

"Despite everything? I don't—I don't remind you of bad things?" Adam asks.

"Luis said, the last time I saw him, that there are good things and bad things, and you have to live through both." Tao pauses. "And we lived through a bad thing. This is our good thing. If you want it."

"I do. Want it. So much. I want to get to know you, Tao. This isn't—it isn't what I planned for us, but gods, I don't want to throw it away," Adam says.

"Can you kiss me?" Tao asks, desperately wanting confirmation—to remember how it felt to be touched and not to be afraid.

Adam moves carefully so he doesn't jostle Tao's head. He leans down and presses a small kiss to Tao's lips. Tao smiles into it, and Adam does too. It's simple and chaste, but it means everything. It's a promise of more to come.

When Adam pulls away, Tao asks the last question they'd been putting off, the one that hurts the most, the one that acknowledges it all.

"Did Pru get to her grandparents?"

"Yeah," Adam says. "When Zeke came to get you, I insisted he take her too. He took her. Stayed for the whole thing. They cremated her. I think she would have wanted that."

"She didn't want to be brought back," Tao remembers.

"Yeah," Adam says. "She's with her parents now. She's home."

"Is it bad that I miss her?" Tao tries not to cry and fails, just a little. There will be more tears later, in the days and weeks and months to come, but for now there's this.

"I think it'd be weird if you didn't. She meant a lot to you. You can still miss people, even if they hurt you," Adam says and presses a kiss to Tao's shoulder. "You can miss her forever, and that'd be okay."

"I don't know how to deal with what happened," Tao says.

"Time," Adam says. "That's what Zeke told me. Just time. There's no right or wrong way to mourn, to heal. It all just takes time."

"Okay," Tao says and then yawns.

They let their eyes fall closed again and feel Adam curl around them. The darkness carries them away once more, but it's okay. They have time.

EPILOGUE

Two Years Later

TAO LOOKS over at Adam, at the freckles that dot like constellations over his shoulders, his cheeks, even the tips of his ears. In the light of the early morning sun, slatted by the half-open blinds, Adam looks like a minor god, his skin more tan than it has ever been, the old scars on his chest faded.

Tao is as in love as they've ever been, perhaps more so, as they watch Adam drift back to consciousness and smile as he makes a rather undignified noise with his nose as he crosses from sleeping to awake.

"Were you watching me sleep again?" He rolls over to prop himself up on one elbow and meet Tao's eyes.

"It's hard not to," Tao says. "Look at you. How do I get to have this?"

Adam's hair is unruly where he's slept on it, and without his glasses, he squints a little. It's almost too adorable for Tao to bear.

"What time is it?" Adam asks. Tao doesn't bother checking.

"Still early," they say.

"That's good." Adam smiles and wraps his calves around Tao's to pull them closer. "Any plans for the day?"

"I thought we could go to the beach later," Tao says, and they smile as Adam runs a finger down their side, over ribs, and to the jut of their hip bone.

"That sounds nice." Adam smiles lazily. He leans up and presses a kiss to the closest part of Tao he can reach—Tao's chin—and Tao shifts so their mouths find each other.

Adam leaves little nipping kisses on Tao's lips and then pulls away.

"Your morning breath is terrible," he remarks, and Tao barks out a laugh and shoves at him.

"Yours isn't any better," they say, "and besides, you snore."

Adam smiles that lazy smile again and falls back into the pillows.

Tao rests their head on the flat of his chest and listens to the steady thrum of his heartbeat. They've used its gentle rhythm to drift off to sleep so many times.

This is their life now, for the time being. They move around a lot—from towns to cities to villages—but for now, this small life by the coast belongs to them.

It seems so far removed from everything they knew, and maybe that's okay.

"Do you ever think we could ever stay somewhere?" they ask, and Adam runs lazy fingers through their hair.

"You like it here," he says—a statement, not a question.

"Yeah," Tao says. "I do."

"We can stay as long as you like," he says. "We have time."

Tao moves their head slightly so they can look around the room, at the clutter they've accumulated through their travels—Adam's stacks of books, Mary Mallon's journals prominent among them, liberated before they left Nomos. They have *stuff*, and their small house is full of the life they've built.

It's the first place where they've felt like they could put down roots.

"You're thinking really hard," Adam says quietly and strokes down their cheek to touch the tattoos there. No new ones since Nomos, no more blood spilled.

"Just happy to be here," they say, and their eyes catch the flower painting—blue and bold on the wall opposite, packed full of protective energy—the first thing they did when they moved in.

"I'm happy you're here," Adam says and presses a kiss to their forehead. "I'm happy we're both here."

We made it. We survived.

There are years to come, each of them complicated in their own ways, but Tao looks forward, resting in the arms of the boy they love.

They look at the painting.

Forget-me-nots.

They smile and return their attention to Adam.

The sun washes in, lights them up, warms their bare skin.

"I love you," they say, and they've said it hundreds of times over the past two years, maybe thousands. It never feels like enough.

"I love you too," Adam says, and it's so easy.

It wasn't, and it won't be, but that's okay.

They have all the time in the world to figure it out, and besides, the universe is rooting for them.

THE END

CHARLOTTE AMELIA POE (they/them) is a thirty-three-year-old British author and artist. After winning the Spectrum Art Award in 2018, they published their memoir, How To Be Autistic, in 2019. That book won the East Anglian Book Award for Biography and Memoir and was runner up for the ALCS Educational Award. *How To Be Autistic* has since been optioned as a television series and translated into Spanish and Brazilian Portuguese. *The Language of Dead Flowers* is Poe's first novel and explores the three genders - man, woman, and necromancer (this is a little gender joke for the nonbinaries out there). Poe is a bisexual, asexual, autistic, nonbinary disaster and enjoys browsing tumblr, reading fanfiction, and going to comic cons. Poe can be found at @smallreprieves on Instagram, following pretty people, and @charlottepoe on Twitter. They live in a tiny village with their family and two dogs. They are a little bit obsessed with Taylor Swift and eagerly await the Reputation re-record. In the meantime, they can be found writing and complaining about writing (perhaps one more than the other).

THE PRINCE
AND THE
ICE KING

A Tale from the Gemstone Kingdoms

AMANDA MEUWISSEN

Book One of Tales from the Gemstone Kingdoms

Every Winter Solstice, the Emerald Kingdom sends the dreaded Ice King a sacrifice—a corrupt soul, a criminal, a deviant, or someone touched by magic. Prince Reardon has always loathed this tradition, partly because he dreams of love with another man instead of a future queen.

Then Reardon's best friend is discovered as a witch and sent to the Frozen Kingdom as tribute.

Reardon sets out to rescue him, willing to battle and kill the Ice King if that's what it takes. But nothing could prepare him for what he finds in the Frozen Kingdom—a cursed land filled with magic… and a camaraderie Reardon has never known. Over this strange, warm community presides the enigmatic Ice King himself, a man his subjects call Jack. A man with skin made of ice, whose very touch can stop a beating heart.

A man Reardon finds himself inexplicably drawn to.

Jack doesn't trust Reardon. But when Reardon begins spending long days with him, vowing to prove himself and break the curse, Jack begins to hope. Can love and forgiveness melt the ice around Jack's heart?

www.dreamspinnerpress.com

STITCHES

A Tale from the Gemstone Kingdoms

AMANDA MEUWISSEN

Book Two of Tales from the Gemstone Kingdoms

Created by the alchemist Braxton, Levi was "born" fully grown and spends his early days learning about the monster-filled kingdom he calls home.

Even though he is just a construct pieced together from cloned parts, Levi longs to fit in with his mythical neighbors, but more than that, he wishes he could say two words to the Shadow King without stuttering.

Ashmedai has been king of what was once the Amethyst Kingdom since it was cursed a thousand years ago. Only he and Braxton know what truly happened the night of the curse, and Ash's secret makes walking among his beloved people painful, so he rarely leaves his castle. However, with Festival Day approaching, Ash wouldn't mind going out more often... if it means seeing more of Levi.

Ash wishes he deserved the longing looks from those strangely familiar violet eyes. He knows no one could love him after learning the truth of the curse. But if anyone can change his mind, it is the sweetly stitched young man who looks at him like he hung the moon.

www.dreamspinnerpress.com

The Wanderer

Rowan McAllister

Chronicles of the Riftlands: Book One

After centuries of traveling the continent of Kita and fighting the extradimensional monsters known as Riftspawn, mage Lyuc is tired and ready to back away from the concerns of humanity.

But the world isn't done with him yet.

While traveling with a merchant caravan, Lyuc encounters Yan, an Unnamed, the lowest caste in society. Though Yan has nothing but his determination and spirit, he reminds Lyuc what passion and desire feel like. While wild magic, a snarky, shapeshifting, genderfluid companion, and the plots of men and monsters seem determined to keep Lyuc from laying down his burden, only Yan's inimitable spirit tempts him to hang on for another lifetime or so.

All Yan wants is to earn the sponsorship of a guild so he can rise above his station, claim a place in society, and build the family he never had.

After hundreds of years of self-imposed penance, all Lyuc wants is Yan.

If they can survive prejudice, bandits, mercenaries, monsters, and nature itself, they might both get their wish… and maybe even their happily ever after.

www.dreamspinnerpress.com

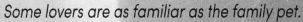
Some lovers are as familiar as the family pet.

FAMILIAR
ANGEL

Amy Lane

"Fantastic...a transcendent
love story that will sweep you
off your feet."
CINDY DEES,
NYT and *USA Today*
Bestselling Author

"Both striking and sensual"
Publishers Weekly

Familiar Love: Book One

One hundred and forty years ago, Harry, Edward, and Francis met an angel, a demon, and a sorceress while escaping imprisonment and worse! They emerged with a new family—and shapeshifting powers beyond their wildest dreams.

Now Harry and his brothers use their sorcery to rescue those enslaved in human trafficking—but Harry's not doing so well. Pining for Suriel the angel has driven him to take more and more risks until his family desperately asks Suriel for an intervention.

In order for Suriel to escape the bindings of heaven, he needs to be sure enough of his love to fight to be with Harry. Back when they first met, Harry was feral and angry, and he didn't know enough about love for Suriel to justify that risk. Can Suriel trust in Harry enough now to break his bonds of service for the boy who has loved his Familiar Angel for nearly a century and a half?

www.dreamspinnerpress.com

Amy Lane

FAMILIAR DEMON

Familiar Love: Book Two

For over a century, Edward Youngblood has been the logical one in a family of temperamental magical beings. But reason has not made him immune to passion, and Edward's passion for Mullins, the family's demon instructor, has only grown.

Mullins was lured into hell through desperation—and a fatal mistake. He's done his best to hang onto his soul in the twisted realm of the underworld, and serving the Youngblood family when summoned has been his only joy. Edward concocts a plan to spring Mullins by collecting a series of items to perform an ancient ritual—an idea that terrifies Mullins. He can't bear the thought of losing Edward and his brothers to a dangerous quest.

But every item in their collection is an adventure in brotherhood and magic, and as Mullins watches from the sidelines, he becomes more and more hopeful that they will succeed. When the time comes for Mullins to join the mission, can he find enough faith and hope to redeem himself and allow himself happiness in the arms of a man who would literally go to hell and back—and beyond—to have Mullins by his side?

www.dreamspinnerpress.com